QUENTIN JAM

QUENTIN JAMES ar

QUENTIN JAMES

QUENTIN JAMES and the JACOBITE GOLD

QUENTIN JAMES and the GLOBAL WAR GAMES
CYBER SLEUTHS
Bug Wars/Zombie Wars
A Quentin James companion adventure

QUENTIN JAMES and the ARCTIC ADVENTURE
QUENTIN JAMES and the BATTLE for EDGEWATER

*

THE PRINCE OF LIGHT:

WITCHES" EYE
CASTLE ADVENTUROUS
THE QUEEN OF MAGIC

*

OTHER TITLES

EBENEZER

*

THE LIBRARY
THE LIBRARY: AUGUSTUS

*

THE O'BRIEN DETECTIVE AGENCY

*

THE DEMON HUNTERS
(Adults Only)
The Borley Rectory
JACK

ACKNOWLEDGEMENTS

With thanks to the excellent resources of

Richard Jones's

Jack The Ripper 1888.
The Whitechapel Murders History Resource
http://jack-the-ripper.org

*

Ryder, Stephen P. (Ed.)

'Casebook: Jack the Ripper.'
http://www.casebook.org

*

Rupert Matthews.
Jack the Ripper, Streets of Terror

*

And
Maria Wilson
For braving the first read.

ENGLAND
January 1888

'Brrrrrrrrrr, it's perishing. Why have you brought me here?' asked Adriana, pulling her hat down further before grasping her coat tighter. 'I cannot see a thing in this fog.'

'London, England,' said Shaun.

'England again? Can't we investigate ghostly sightings somewhere warm?'

'We're not here for ghosts this time Riana, not this time.'

Warmth flooded her body, and she smiled.

'Come on, if we're quick we can save a man's life.'

Adriana's focus snapped back to her surrounds, and she raced after Shaun, the fog barely moving as she ran along the path. A loud *crack,* like a pistol shot, filled the air, followed by a cry.

It was impossible to see more than a foot in front of their faces so the first she knew of the canal was when Shaun slipped on the ice and landed with a thud, followed by a snap and crackle as a crack snaked across the surface.

'We have to be quick,' said Shaun, his feet scrabbling on the icy surface as he heaved himself up, Adriana pulling on his arm, though compared to the muscled bulk of Shaun, her elfin frame offered little by way of assistance.

Shaun and Adriana moved along the edge of the canal as fast as they dared, their eyes straining within the freezing fog.

'There!' Adriana cried out, letting go of Shaun and stepping out onto the ice.

Pain shot through her hand as she plunged it into the icy depths and grabbed the thick material of a coat. Shaun was beside her instantly and together they heaved and hauled the man up out of the water. Other hands joined theirs and together they pulled the man to the side of the canal and up onto the bank.

It was too late. The man's skin was gray, the eyes lifeless.

'That's Bill, the postman,' said one voice.

'Aye, tis a shame. Water must be as cold as ice. Never stood a chance,' said another.

Shaun slipped his fingers over the postman's eyes, closing them for the last time before bowing his head.

Adriana bowed hers in prayer as Shaun said a few words entreating God to take the man into his embrace.

'Amen.'

'Amen.'

Shaun pushed himself to his feet and, holding out his hand, helped Adriana to stand.

'Come, we have to get back,' said Shaun.

Adriana looked at Shaun in surprise before nodding, waiting until they were out of earshot before asking, 'Back?'

Shaun nodded.

'We are in the right time, the right year. I need to bring you up to speed on where we are and what we're about.'

'I get to know in advance? I thought you preferred me to be unbiased by the historical events.'

'Usually yes, but this time it would be too dangerous.'

Adriana felt the pull of the time gate and her step quickened unconsciously.

'That's sounds ominous, what year is this?'

'1888.'

WHITECHAPEL
March 1888

Adriana's brow furrowed as she searched her memory, frustration coursing through her, not for the first time, at the gaps within her mind, where all personal information about who she was, where she came from, grew up; family and so on, was missing. Her first memories of self were waking up in a field a little ways away from a convent, which had taken her in, tended to her injuries, and aided her recovery. The rest of her memories, names, faces, facts, and friends and so on, were perfectly retrievable.

'1888? That's ringing a bell. Great Fire of London?'

Shaun shook his head, 'That was 1666, close though.'

Adriana laughed. 'If you call 222 years close.'

Shaun laughed. 'True. Let me add the place; Whitechapel.'

Adriana's smile disappeared. 'Whitechapel?'

Shaun nodded. 'He was never found. He came out of nowhere and disappeared the same way.'

'And he was possessed by a Demon?'

Shaun leafed through sheets of paper before handing one to Adriana.

'That's what we're going to find out.'

Adriana took the sheet and looked at the title;

Jack the Ripper 1888

The Whitechapel Murders History Resource

Site Author – Richard Jones.

'Something brought this man into the dark of evil and just as quickly left him. If we can find him, we can save his soul and maybe the lives of some of his victims.'

Adriana nodded. 'Where do we start?'

'Whitechapel. We need to learn all we can about the time and the place.'

Adriana moved to her favourite seat in the room they were using as their office. A room of walls filled floor to ceiling with bookshelves, crammed full of books and papers. A large desk dominated the floor space, shared by them both, with chairs and laptops either side. In one corner sat the only comfy chair, an old battered leather armchair she loved.

Curling her legs beneath her, she waited for Shaun to start, smiling gently as he cleared his throat several times, shuffled his papers, tugged at this collar, and rolled his shoulders before looking up.

She squeezed her body tight in a self-hug enjoying the rush of tingles as his eyes met hers, widened as they always did, a faint blush suffusing his cheeks.

He cleared his throat again.

'I've been reading up on Whitechapel in 1888, a book called Jack the Ripper's Streets of Terror helped me get a sense of what London was like during that year. It's where I read about the death of the Postman, falling into the canal. I had hoped we could get to him in time.'

Adriana waited in shared silence as Shaun closed his eyes for a moment.

'So what do we know about 1888? It started out cold, very cold, freezing fog covered the city, closing down the ports. Heavy snow fell across the country and everything ground to halt, London included, with held the largest population in the world at that time with its six million souls.'

Adriana was quickly scanning the book on her kindle.

'The underground was running in the eighteen hundreds?' she said surprised.

Shaun nodded.

'The Circle line was the first of the Underground lines up and running, even Whitechapel was accessible by the underground then, and you have to remember this was an impoverished area of London.'

'Come, let's take a walk along Whitechapel and see what's there today.

*

'It is interesting,' said Shaun, 'that Whitechapel is so named because of a White Chapel that used to exist on the old Roman Road running east outside the then, city limits. As the City grew it enveloped the area but the name stuck and still exists today.'

Adriana stopped.

'Can you feel that?'

'Seems like we have a time window,' said Shaun.

'Time gate,' corrected Adriana. 'I think of them as time gates.'

Shaun considered this for a moment and then shrugged, 'Sounds good to me, Time Gate it is.'

Adriana wrapped a scarf around her neck and pulled a hat from her bag, a shiver from the anticipated cold running down her back.

'If it doesn't warm up, I will have to go shopping for some thermals,' she said.

'It might not be early January this time,' said Shaun.

'Here's hoping.'

Shaun stepped through, Adriana a step behind.

*

'Phew, that's a relief,' said Adriana, looking about her. 'It's a lot warmer than before?'

'Sister? Father? It is a pleasure to meet you both,' said a man standing on the corner.

Adriana jumped in surprise and then glared at Shaun as he chuckled.

'Good afternoon, Father, I'm Father Shaun, this is Sister Adriana.'

'How do you do? I am a Canon actually, Canon Barnet.'

'My apologies, Canon, I didn't realise.'

The Canon waved his hand dismissively.

'It is of no matter. You mentioned it was cold the last time you were here?'

Shaun nodded. 'We were last here in January.'

'Oh my, yes, that was quite the cold snap we had. Freezing fog and snow. It's warmer now the spring is here.'

Adriana watched as two policemen met at the corner of the street.

'They look deep in conversation, what are they are talking about I wonder?' said Adriana.

'Oh, they all do that,' said the Canon. The streets are all patrolled and when two policemen meet, they share information. That way they are aware of what's happening all around.'

'That would be very useful. What about them, what are they doing?' Adriana asked, nodding her head towards two men standing outside a shop.

'Those, they are Vigilants. The shop employs then to keep the peace, watch out for pick pockets or trouble from the gangs.'

'Gangs?'

'Yes the Hip Rip gangs.'

'I understood the Hip Rip Gang was based in Liverpool,' said Shaun.

Adriana looked at Shaun in amazement.

'What? I read,' said Shaun, with a smile.

The Canon nodded. 'You are correct, Father, but some of the local youth gangs have adopted the name.'

'So it's a rough area, Whitechapel?' said Adriana.

The Canon shook his head.

'Not the whole area no, but it has it sections just like any other.'

Shaun nodded, looking down the street thoughtfully.

'Well, thank you, Canon, we won't keep you, you must be a busy man.'

'Yes, quite. Thank you. A good day to you both.'

'A good day to you, Canon.'

Adriana and Shaun watched the Canon as he walked down the street for a minute or two, both digesting all they had been told.

'Come, let us return, and prepare,' said Shaun.

Adriana looked at Shaun in surprise.

'I'm not getting the usual tug of a Time Gate, can you feel it?'

Shaun nodded and, taking her gently by the arm, steered her down an alley.

The coldness rippled through them as they stepped through the invisible curtain in time and found themselves still in the alley.

'That's odd,' said Adriana.

EMMA SMITH
3rd April 1888

'Come on,' said Shaun.

Adriana was startled as Shaun took off at a run but was soon hot on his heels.

Through the streets they raced.

'George Street,' Shaun yelled, pointing as he veered left. 'We want number 18.'

Moments later Shaun was pounding on the door.

'Emma Smith, where is she?' he demanded, the moment the door opened.

'Her room is on the top floor,' said the woman who opened the door.

Shaun pushed past her and took the stairs two at a time.

'Here, you can't barge in just like that.'

'It's ok, Miss...?'

'Russell, Mary Russell.'

'Miss Russell, he's a priest. I'm a nun, we're here to help.'

'Adriana!'

Adriana looked up as Shaun called out her name and pushed past the old lady, and, noticing the blood on the steps, lifted the skirts of her habit as she hastened upstairs.

She gasped as she entered the room.

The lady on the bed looked awful. Her face had been battered and was bleeding profusely from several cuts as well as from her nose, lips and mouth, her ear had been cut and she was crying softly.

Shaun held her tenderly, dabbing at the cuts softly with his handkerchief.

'We have to get her to hospital,' he said quietly.

'Emma? Emma? My name is Sister Adriana, and this is Father Shaun. We are here to help you. We are going to help you stand and get you to the hospital.'

Emma nodded, gasping as she swung one leg off the bed.

'Gently now, there's no rush. We have plenty of time,' said Shaun soothingly.

Adriana nodded and together they helped Emma stand, their hands gentle on her arms, already black and purple with bruises.

As they helped her down the stairs. 'Where's the nearest hospital?' Shaun asked.

'That'll be the London, on Whitechapel Road,' said the old woman, one hand on the door, the other covering her mouth, the horror clear in her eyes.

'Who would do such a thing?' she whispered.

Adriana shook her head, not trusting her voice, her vision blurred through unshed tears. She looked over at Shaun desperately hoping he would ease her sorrow, tell her Emma would live but he steadfastly looked ahead, refusing to meet her gaze.

Once on the street Shaun picked Emma up into his arms and easily carried her as he hurried along the road.

*

'There is nothing more we can do here,' said Shaun. 'Emma said she was attacked by a group of men on Osborn Street. Let's go and check it out.'

Adriana nodded, her blood boiling, her thoughts less than godly at that moment.

As they walked along Wentworth Street, Shaun stiffened and Adriana followed his gaze across the road where a group of men were loitering, some leaning against the wall, others milling about restless, clearly anxious. One caught Adriana's gaze and leered.

Adriana quickly averted her eyes and grabbed Shaun's arm as he made to cross and confront them.

'Leave them,' she said, her voice trembling. 'Look, there's Osborn Street.'

Shaun pulled his gaze away from the gang and looked down a narrow dirty street.

'What happens?' Adriana asked quietly.

'She dies,' said Shaun, looking across the road once more, his hands clenched into fists.

'Why is this murder important? Is it related to Jack the Ripper?'

Turning, she looked across the road at the gang more intently.

'Is one of them Jack?'

Shaun shook his head.

'No. They're just one of the High Rip Gangs Canon Barnet told us about. They robbed and beat Emma and committed an indecent assault that will lead to her death but Jack is not amongst them.'

'Indecent assault?'

Shaun looked at Adriana. 'The details are unimportant.'

'They might be; we don't know at this stage what is important and what is not. I appreciate you are trying to protect me but from what little I read of Jack the Ripper, this case is going to get far uglier than Emma.'

Shaun nodded and took a moment.

'They shoved something blunt into her vagina, so hard it ruptured something deep inside and she died of peritonitis, an inflammation of the lining, treatable in our day but here...now.....'

Shaun looked sad and angry at the same time and his body tensed once again as some of the gang members stirred and sneered at them from across the road.

Adriana's tummy roiled as her thoughts turned over the new details of the murder, coupled with the images of poor Emma lying on her bed covered in blood.

'Any witnesses?'

Shaun shook his head.

'The inquest will record that the Constables on duty in the area, saw or heard nothing and no one came forward as a witness. There were no Constables about when we took Emma to the hospital. I was looking out for one, and we must have been quite the sight.'

Adriana nodded thoughtfully.

'So, despite the number of Constables on the beat, together with the Vigilants, it is still possible for such events to go unnoticed.'

Shaun looked at Adriana and nodded.

'That's a good point. Could go a long way in explaining how Jack was able to commit murder and escape without so much as a chase or sighting.'

Adriana took an involuntary step down the narrow street, shrouded in gloom despite the sun shining.

'I feel it too,' said Shaun. 'Come on.'

Together they entered, what to Adriana was little more than an alleyway then a street, and the coldness washed over them.

MARTHA TABRAM
7ᵗʰ August 1888

'You asked why Emma's murder was important,' said Shaun. 'Whilst it's considered unrelated to the Ripper murders, it was the first of what was known as the Whitechapel Murders.'

'So there are other murders then? Ones that occur in Whitechapel but not thought to be by Jack the Ripper?'

Shaun nodded. 'Seven others were recorded, some before, most after the five attributed to the Ripper, twelve in all.'

'Twelve murders just in Whitechapel, all within, what, a year?' said Adriana. 'Something has to be behind that.'

'That's my thinking. Though the murders span four years, only five were attributed to the Ripper, of the other seven, one was killed in 1887, the others span 1888 through to 1891. If we can find out who or what is behind them, we might stop the Ripper before he gets started.'

'Where are we heading?'

'A place known as George Yard, one of the most dangerous streets in London according to newspapers of the time, so be weary.'

Adriana nodded.

'One other thing Emma mentioned, was that one of her attackers looked about nineteen,' said Shaun.

'Is that significant?'

'Could be,' Shaun said, nodding his head forwards.

Adriana looked ahead and across the street where a young man stood watching them, biting his nails. The moment their eyes connected he bolted.

'Well that's suspicious. Why is he watching us?'

'I am pretty sure he was with the High Rip gang we saw on Wentworth Street,' said Shaun. 'Whether he is watching or perhaps waiting for us I'm not sure.'

'Waiting for us?'

Shaun nodded. 'I cannot be positive but I get the impression that young man has something on his mind he would like to share.'

As they approached the top of the street known as George Yard, quite a crowd had gathered. Police Constables were taking notes from several people and Shaun steered Adriana around so they were close enough to listen.

'So, Mrs Hewitt, you came home around what time?'

'I don't know for sure, it was late, I'd been out drinking with friends, so was a little worse for wear I can tell you. Didn't see a thing. I went out again, bit later, to get a bite to eat, and still didn't see her. It turns my insides cold it does, to think of that poor girl lying there as I walked passed.'

'Did you hear anything, Mrs Hewitt, once you were home?'

'Not a thing. My husband and I sleep like logs. Nothing short of an earthquake is going to wake us once we are asleep.'

'Thank you, Mrs Hewitt, that should be all for now. I might have some more questions for you later.'

Noticing Shaun moving a little closer to another witness, Adriana followed.

'Your name please, sir?'

'Crow, Constable, Alfred George Crow.'

'Occupation?'

'Cab driver.'

'And do you live hereabouts sir?'

'I do, number 35 George Yard Buildings.'

'And what time did you return home last night Mr Crow?'

'About half past three, this morning.'

'And did you see Miss Tabram?'

'Well, I didn't know her name then, but I did see her lying on the first floor landing. That is quite common ya know, so I didn't think anything of it. I thought she was asleep is all.'

Adriana's attention was drawn to another Police Constable.

'So you found the body, Mr Reeves?'

'Yes, Sir, I was on my way to work when I saw her lying there, at first I thought she was sleeping, I did, but then I noticed all the blood you see.'

'And what did you do next?'

'I went and found Mr Barrett I did. I told him, I did, I told him I found a dead girl.'

'Do you know Constable Barrett?'

'Everyone round here knows Mr Barrett. Good man he is.'

'And about what time would this be, Mr Reeves?'

'Bout 5 it was, I always leave for work bout 5 I do.'

'And where is it you work, Sir?'

'I work at the Waterside I do, I'm a labour you see.'

'Thank you, Mr Reeves.'

'I fetched the Doc like I was asked, I did,' said Mr Reeves, pointing to a man standing with a couple of Constables.

'Yes, Sir, thank you for that,' said the Constable, patting Mr Reeves on the arm.

Adriana tugged Shaun's sleeve and together they moved around, slipping through the crowd to get closer to the Doctor.

'We'll have to wait for my full examination of course,' said the Doctor. 'But I've never seen anything like it.'

'Can you say if it was rape, Dr Killeen?'

'Not from my initial examination no. Of course Miss Tabram is a known prostitute in the area, often seen with another girl, goes by the name Pearly Poll.'

'Pearly Poll?' asked one man, standing next to the Constables.

'Yes Inspector, Mary Ann Connolly, known in the area. Good girl, often seen with Martha,' said one of the Constables.

'Prostitute?'

'Yes, Inspector.'

'Have we spoken to her yet?'

'Yes, Sir.'

The Constable looked through his notes.

'Poll said, she and Martha were in several pubs along the Whitechapel Road and they met a couple of guardsmen along the way.'

'Have we identified who these guardsmen are?'

'No, sir, not yet.'

'Anything else?'

'Well, Sir, this area is often used for a four penny, if you know what I mean.'

'I do, Constable, go on.'

'Martha brought one of the guardsmen back here, whilst Poll took hers to Angel Alley.'

'Angel Alley?'

'Yes Sir, it's the next street along. Just as dark and private as this one.'

'This makes the guardsmen our prime suspects.'

'Yes, Sir.'

'Identifying the guardsmen is our top priority.'

'Yes, Sir.'

'Inspector Dew?'

'That will be all, Constable. Yes, Doctor?'

'I can tell you that the wounds were inflicted by two different blades.'

'Are you sure, Doctor?'

'Yes Sir, most of them are shallow, but there is a much deeper wound on her breast. It's speculation but it could be from a bayonet.'

'Thank you, Doctor.'

Shaun looked at Adriana.

'Let's go,' he said.

Together, they moved through the crowd and down the street, both silent as they absorbed the barbarity of the murder.

'I was surprised so many women were there,' said Adriana.

Shaun was startled out of his thoughts.

'What? Women?'

'Yes, in the crowd.'

Shaun nodded. 'Understandable given the victim was a woman, and most of the men will be at work.'

Adriana pursed her lips before nodding.

'There's that boy again,' she said.

Shaun looked around before seeing the young man standing at the corner.

Their eyes met, and the boy hesitated for just a moment before turning and running around the corner out of sight.

'He definitely has something on his mind,' said Shaun.

Adriana nodded then gasped and found herself standing in their shared office.

'Wow, I had no warning.'

Shaun barely heard her as he moved to his desk and started rifling through the papers scattered across the surface.

'We need to find something, anything that can lead us to the Ripper before he kills again.'

'So Martha was killed by Jack?'

'I am not sure, part of me says yes, but another says no, it's all mixed up.'

Adriana took her seat on the other side of the desk, grabbed a pen, and started to write furiously.

'What are you writing?'

'Everything. If there is something not in the historical records, it might just be the clue we need. Now ssssshhh, let me think.'

Shaun sat down to make notes of his own.

So occupied with her thoughts, Adriana didn't think to question how the time gate had placed them, not at the location of George's Yard but within their own office.

MARY NICHOLS
31ˢᵗ August 1888

'Get out.'

'Please, I have nowhere else to sleep.'

'Not my problem. 4pence a bed, take it or leave it.'

The shadow moved in the darkness, watching, waiting. Fingers curled and uncurled around the handle of the knife, heart pounding, mouth dry, shifting in anticipation as the woman pulled her shawl around her shoulders tighter and stepped out into the street.

The thrill tingled, breathing shortened as the shadow flowed along behind the woman, confident she was unaware of its presents as it blended with the darkness.

She turned off the Whitechapel Road onto Buck's Row.

The street was narrow with tall buildings either side, the black of night dominated the area, broken only by the odd street lamp, their light meagre, offering little comfort to the woman but welcomed by the shadow that moved closer.

A glint of metal flashed as it slowly pulled a blade from beneath the black clock before slipping back.

It was too soon for the knife.

With a leap, the shadow was on the woman, the surprise, and additional weight taking them both to the ground. Any cry, silenced, as hands slipped around her throat and squeezed.

Looking into her eyes, seeing them widen in fear, seeing the shock register as the woman gazed upon the visage of her murderer, her need to breathe becoming desperate. Intoxicated, the shadow could feel the life leaving as her pulse slowed, and revelled in it.

Fear tinged the excitement the coursed through its body; arousal tightened the groin as the blade cut deep, sliding across the woman's throat shockingly easily. Quickly now, the token, the offering must be gathered. Skirts were raised, pushed high to expose her stomach, the knife slicing, cutting, parting the skin. Hands dived into the opening, fumbling.

A sound, a scuff nothing more, alerted the murderer. Grabbing the knife, the shadow melted away into the blackness, leaving the woman lying in the gateway.

Eyes followed a man as he walked up the street, breath held as the man bent down to look at the victim, frustration boiled as another man walked up the road.

'Come and look over here, there is a woman lying on the pavement.'

The first man touched her face.

'It's warm.'

He held her hand by the forearm, showing the second man how limp it was.

'Hands are cold though, I believe she is dead.'

'I think she is breathing,' said the second man, 'but very little if she is.'

The darkness moved, agitated. It had been so perfect, so easy, only to be disturbed by these two men. Trapped, unable to move for fear of being seen, the need to move was pressing, to escape, to flee the scene, to run. RUN!

'Let's sit her up.'

'I'm not touching her,' said the first man, standing and looking up and down the street. 'I'm late for work. We'll tell the first policeman we see.'

The second man pulled her skirts down.

'Aye, me too.'

The darkness stepped out onto the street, watching the two men hurry off before walking in the opposite direction, unhurried, the agitation and frustration, almost overwhelming just moments before, evaporating as the excitement returned, the thrill of getting away with murder coursed throughout the body, tightening loins and shortening breath. The only troubling thought was the lack of tribute, the trophy it had failed to obtain.

MARY NICHOLS
31ˢᵗ August 2017

'Ok, this is it, this is Bucks Row of old,' said Shaun. 'It's been renamed Durward Street, but this is the place.'

'How can you be sure?' asked Adriana.

Shaun pointed to the large imposing building.

'That was the boarding school. Flats now, but back in 1888 that school stood exactly as it does today, bout the only thing left, actually. See those railings at the top; they enclosed the school playground. I'll show you a photo taken back in the 1900s, and you can just make out those same railings.'

Adriana gave a shiver.

'You can feel it, right? The creepiness?'

Shaun nodded.

'Some crimes leave a tear in time, the evil seeps through, chilling the air forever. So, just here, this is where the murder took place.'

Adriana moved to stand next to Shaun, just in front of a wall on a patch of open ground.

'So Charles Cross was the first to find the body around 3:40am on August 31st 1888.'

Adriana looked at Shaun. 'I'm guessing it's no coincidence we're standing here.' Adrian paused whilst she did some maths. 'Over one hundred years later.'

Shaun shook his head. 'Charles saw the body as a misshapen heap and mistook it for some tarpaulin. When he got closer, he realised it was the body of a woman. Mary Nichols. Not that he knew her name at that moment of course. A second man comes along, Robert Paul, who he beckons over and together they check the body. Now Charles notes that whilst the face is warm, the hands are cold, and Robert, on touching her chest, feels it move, believes she is breathing, although shallowly.'

'So she was alive when they found her,' said Adriana.

Shaun shook his head. 'No, they didn't see it in the darkness, but her throat had been cut so deep her head was barely attached to the body.'

Adriana shivered.

'So what did they do?'

'They pulled her skirts down and continued on to work.'

'What!'

'To their credit, they planned on telling the first policeman they met.'

'To their credit! They left the poor girl lying dead in the street and continued on their journey to work! As if, as if...'

Shaun placed his hand on Adriana's shoulder.

'Do not judge them too harshly, at least not yet.'

Adriana looked at Shaun sharply.

'You suspect one of these men is the Ripper.'

Shaun nodded.

'Both were on their way to work, which explains why they were both walking along the street in the early hours of the morning. But her face was warm, hands cold which tells us she had died moments before she was discovered, certainly not an hour before, less, a lot less.'

'So Charles could have killed her, but, disturbed by Robert, quickly called him over, providing himself with an alibi, that they had discovered the body together, more or less,' said Adriana

Shaun nodded.

'And suggesting they leave the body and continue on to work, was his escape.'

'In one report I read, they didn't tell the Police either,' continued Shaun. 'A PC John Neil discovered the body whilst doing his rounds and he reported that he had walked pass this very spot not thirty minutes earlier and saw no one, and there was no body, yet on his next pass, there she was, lying on the ground. With the aid of his lamp he could see all the blood and discovered the cause of death, her throat being cut, he also noted her eyes were wide open.'

Adriana crossed herself, eyes closed as she said a small prayer; her eyes snapping open as the tug of a time gate pull her so strongly she took a step or two.

Taking the offered hand of Shaun's they stepped through, coldness rippling down her body.

Adriana looked up at the imposing bulk of the boarding school, only, this time, it stood in a street lined with warehouses along one side, and two story houses the other.

Without being told, she knew she was now in 1888, at the scene of Mary Nichols's murder.

MARY NICHOLS
31st August 1888

'Come on, let's go. We can tell the first policeman we see about her.'

Adriana watched as the two men walked away from the body, barely distinguishable in the darkness.

Shaun's hand on her shoulder froze her in place just as the blackness moved. More black than the darkness around, it became visible simply because it moved.

Adriana held her breath as it moved up the street.

'Jack the Ripper,' she said, her voice carried softly on an exhale of breath.

'Come on,' said Shaun, slipping out of the doorway onto the street.

Together they moved silently after the fleeing figure.

'He's not exactly hurrying is he?' Adriana whispered.

'It would draw too much attention.'

'He's gone around the corner, quick!' said Adriana, her voice a mixture of a whisper and a squeak.

They reached the end of the street and peered around the corner.

'Where'd he go?'

'I don't know?' said Shaun, stepping out into the street, walking slowly, checking all the doorways and alleyways.

'Look there's light coming from that building,' said Adriana.

They hurried along and entered a yard.

'Oh,' said Adriana, screwing up her nose.

'Good morning gentlemen,' said Shaun, stepping through the smaller door set within the larger one.

'Morning, Sir, how can we help you?'

'There was a murder in Bucks Row and the murderer came this way, did you see him?'

The three men put down their tools and wiped their hands as they approached Shaun.

'A murder you say?' said one man.

'In Bucks Row?' said another.

Shaun nodded.

'I'm Father Shaun,' said Shaun, loosening his coat to show his collar, 'and this is Sister Adriana.'

'Harry, Jim, and I'm Charlie,' said Charlie, indicating to the others as he said their names.

'Did you see a man coming past just now?' said Adriana.

The three men looked at each other and shook their heads.

'No, Sister, we saw no one.'

Shaun looked up and down the street, the morning dawn lightening the darkness, revealing more nooks and crannies the Ripper could have hid, watching them as they past. He cocked his head as he heard the clatter of hooves and the rumble of wheels but as it was moving slowly, he dismissed it as a getaway.

'Come on, let's keep looking,' said Adriana, taking Shaun's hand and pulling him out of his thoughts.

'Let's go look,' said Jim.

Charlie and Harry nodded and slipped off their bloody leather aprons, gave their red hands a quick wash in a bucket of cold water and, after locking up, headed off to Buck Row.

Watching them go, Adriana said, 'You know it could have been one of them.'

'I was thinking the same thing, all that blood on their aprons and hands; that could have easily come from Mary Nichols. But we saw only one person, so the other two would have to be covering for their friend.'

'Unless they're all murders? Taking turns and providing each other with an alibi.'

Shaun nodded thoughtfully.

'We will have to explore that possibility. Come on, let's see who else is awake at this time of the morning.'

Adriana quickened her step to catch up with Shaun who had walked away in determination.

In the next street along, they came across another man, a Watchman outside the sewage works.

'Good morning, Watchman. There has been a murder down the street. Have you been on duty all night?' asked Shaun.

'I have,' said the Watchman, looking guarded.

'I'm Father Shaun and this is Sister Adriana.'

The Watchman relaxed visibly.

'Morning, Father, Sister, I'm Mulshaw, Patrick Mulshaw. I have been on duty all night but have the odd nap you know. Murder you say?'

Shaun nodded. 'Perfectly understandable. Yes, over in Buck's Row. About an hour ago now.'

The Watchman frowned. 'An hour ago you say? I was awake then, sure as sure can be and I didn't see or hear anything.'

'Perhaps you were dozing,' said Adriana gently.

The Watchman shook his head vehemently.

'No, Sister, definitely not. Workers you see, they start heading to work around three thirty so I have to be awake, case someone dobs me in and I lose my job.'

'And you saw no one, not even some workers?'

The Watchman shook his head.

'Not then, no, first that comes along this way is usually closer to four, but I'm always alert from three just in case, sure as sure can be.'

Adriana placed a calming hand on the Watchman's arm.

'That's ok; we just wanted to be sure.' A smiled twitched her lips.

The Watchman calmed.

'Buck's Row you say?'

Adriana nodded.

'My shift's over so I'll just have a look see,' he said, and hurried off.

Adriana sighed.

'Why does it draw us in?' she asked aloud. 'Murder, mayhem, accidents, and such? We all stop to look.'

'Inquisitiveness, fear, excitement even,' said Shaun. 'Come on let's go back there ourselves, just in case the Ripper doubled back.'

Adriana nodded and together they walked back to Buck's Row.

*

'Move the body; I want her taken to the Mortuary, to many sightseers here for my liking.'

'Who's that? I like him,' said Adriana.

'That be Dr Llewellyn,' said a woman, standing in the crowd.

Adriana watched as two men lifted the body onto a cart, noticing the blood had soaked the back of her clothing and the small river of blood that snaked along the ground into the gutter. She crossed herself and said a small prayer.

'Amen.'

Ripples of 'Amen,' sounded amongst the crowd and several crossed themselves.

'I thought there would have been more blood.'

Adriana turned to see a man scribbling in a note pad.

'Excuse me?' Adriana said.

'Blood, I would have thought there would have been more. And no witnesses? No one hearing a sound? Look where we are. Those are tenanted houses all down that side,' he said pointing with his pencil. 'Respectable too, they would have heard her screams.'

'And what do you make of that?'

'Not killed here, that's for sure. Most likely killed elsewhere and dumped here.'

Adriana looked back at the scene, considering the reporter's thoughts. Was it possible? If so, where was she killed?

'Come on,' said Shaun.

'Goodbye,' said Adriana, but the reporter was too busy writing furiously to pay her any attention.

'I spoke with the Doctor and he invited us to the mortuary.'

Adriana looked at him in surprise.

'How did you manage that?'

Shaun pulled his coat open to show his collar.

'Comes in handy sometimes. I offered to be there when her father and ex husband show up to identify the body.'

THE MORTUARY
31ˢᵗ August 1888

'So, Doctor, your thoughts?'

'The condition of the body proves that she was killed on the spot she was found. There was no trace of blood anywhere else except the spot where her neck was lying, suggesting her throat was cut whilst she was on the ground.'

'What about the other cuts?' asked Adriana, looking down at Mary's stomach, the gaping wound cleaned of blood.

'I'd say they were done after the throat was cut, once she was dead. The lack of blood suggests the heart had stopped beating so there wouldn't have been any spurting for instance.'

Adriana nodded her understanding.

'And her clothing is sodden with blood. Most of the blood from the neck wound was absorbed by her dress,' the doctor added. 'Arrh, Inspector Spratling, anything to add?'

They all turned as an imposing man walked into the room.

'It was the Inspector here who discovered the disembowelling cut across her abdomen.'

'I've had words with those idiots who washed the body, despite our instructions. They insist they were told to do so,' said the Inspector.

'Well, done is done,' said the Doctor, looking out of the brick shed they stood, to the pile of clothing in the yard.

'Seems everyone is quick to clean up this morning. By the time I got to the murder site, one of the locals had already washed away the blood. So there was nothing I could learn there. We've taken in the three men from the Horse Slaughter's Yard for questioning, as you suggested to the Constable, Father, but they alibi each other and their stories are plausible. I suspect this is the work of the Hip Rip gangs personally.'

'Inspector, how did you identify the body?' asked Shaun

'We canvassed the area and several women came forward and identified her as Polly, who usually had a room on Thrawl Street, and I noticed the mark of the Lambeth Workhouse on her petticoat. Mary Ann Monk, who lives there came in and identified her as Mary Nichols. Apparently Mary lived at the workhouse until May.'

'Any information about her movements the hours before her murder?'

The inspector look at Shaun intently and noticeably dropped his gazed to the white collar about his throat before replying.

'She was seen drinking at the Pan pub on the corner of Thrawl Street around 12:30am and was a little tipsy by all accounts. She returned home but was turned aside by the deputy keeper, as she didn't have her doss money. I spoke with him and he assumed she went off, saying something about her bonnet, to earn it,. Anyway she was last seen outside the grocer's shop on Osborne Street, where it meets Whitechapel Road, by her friend, Emily Holland.'

'It amazes me that the murder escaped unseen,' said Doctor Llewellyn. 'His hands at least would have been covered in blood.'

'Just like the men working at the slaughter house,' said Shaun. 'Perhaps that is what he was counting on. Anyone that sees him would assume he worked at one of many slaughter houses in the area and not give it a thought.'

The Inspector nodded. 'We have had the gangs under observation ever since the murder of Emma Smith and Martha Tabram. We are hoping someone within their ranks will break silence and turn Queen's evidence in exchange for a pardon and perhaps a small reward.'

Shaun nodded thoughtfully. 'What would be their motivation to murder though?'

'These gangs prowl the streets in the early hours of the morning, taking money from the poor, any who refuse are beaten. If they fear their deeds are going to be brought to the attention of the authorities, they silence their victims for good.'

Adriana shivered.

Another policeman entered the small room.

'We have completed taking the statements of the residents along Bucks Row,' he said.

'Very good. Anything to report?'

'Only the lack of anything, Sir.'

'Explain.'

'Well, take Mr Purkess, the manager of the Essex Wharf, opposite the murder site, he didn't see or hear a thing. His wife, whose window overlooks the gateway where Mary was murdered and, according to Mr Purkess, had spent a restless night pacing up and down, also claims not to have seen or heard anything. The same for Mrs

Emma Green, who says she is a light sleeper; and the keeper of the Boarding School who's windows look down on the murder site; even the PC on duty, just fifty yards away, on the gate of the Great Eastern Railway Yard, all heard or saw nothing, not a thing. It doesn't seem possible. It's like he's a ghost or something.'

'Ok, that's enough of that kind of talk. If the press get hold of that, we'll have headlines that we're chasing a ghost or some such and be the laughing stock of the city. But I do agree, it is odd that with so many people in such close proximity to the murder, no one saw or heard anything.'

Shaun looked at Adriana and nodded his head towards the exit.

'Let us know if we can be of any use, Inspector,' Shaun said. 'We will be staying with the local parish priest.'

'Very good, Father.'

ANNIE CHAPMAN
8th September 1888

Shaun exchanged a glance with Adriana as the sound of a soft cry filtered down to the study they sat, within with Parish Rectory.

'Pay it no mind,' said the Vicar. 'My wife has cause to discipline the maid again it seems.'

'Again?' said Adriana.

The Vicar nodded. 'In truth she is not a very good maid, keeps forgetting her place but my wife, good hearted soul that she is, refuses to let her go. Becomes quite vexed with me should I even mentioned it. Now I just let her handle it, despite the fact I have caught her on more than one occasion doing the maid's work, polishing the silver or cleaning and laying the fires, to save the maid from losing her position.'

*

The maid watched as the Vicar's wife stepped into the bath before she picked up the bath brush and moved to the edge.

'Stand and bend over,' the maid commanded.

'Yes, Mistress.'

The Lady of the house obeyed and tensed, expecting the sting of the brush across her bottom, something she was becoming all too familiar with since the maid had shown up at her door all those months ago.

A soft cry escaped as she rose on her tiptoes, not from the hard wooden surface of the brush across her backside but the stiff bristles as they were roughly drawn across her most tenderest of flesh.

'You need to learn to obey,' said the Maid, her arm moving back and forth, as she scrubbed away, the brush never leaving its place between the Lady's thighs.

'Yes, Mistress.'

The Lady squirmed as the bristles scratched and scraped her lips, the pain stung horribly but the sparks of pleasure were mounting, her arousal growing.

The maid noted the change in the Lady's moans and after a furious flurry, pressing the head of the brush hard up against the vaginal lips, she brought the brush out from between the thighs and laid it across the Lady's cheeks firmly, spinning the brush mid swing so its broad flat head landed against the soft whiteness.

*

Shaun and Adriana both looked up at the ceiling at the sound of a "Thwack" sounded out.

The Vicar nodded. 'As the good book says, "For the moment all discipline seems painful rather than pleasant, but later it yields the peaceful fruit of righteousness to those who have been trained by it."'

Shaun nodded, looking over the rim of his cup at Adriana whose gaze was steady and without reproach.

The sounds of spanking lasted a long time and was soon accompanied by cries that rose in volume before they were replaced by other moans entirely.

*

With a bottom of crimson red, the Vicar's wife stepped out of the bath, dropped to her knees and crawled over to where her maid and mistress sat, legs apart, dress drawn up, waiting. Without hesitation, the Lady placed her lips against her Mistress's nether lips and after planting a reverent kiss, licked the soft folds, seeking out the plump bud she knew to give the most pleasure.

Orgasm after orgasm crashed through the maid, her body jerking and clenching in blissful spasms as she was pleasured, her moans loud and unabashed. The Lady's knees hurt, her back ached, and mouth and tongue ached by the time she was pushed away.

'Enough. See me tonight before bed for another spanking,' said the maid, as she rose, settled her dress about her and left the bathroom.

The Lady of the house sat on her heels watching the girl leave with the confidence and assurance she once had, with nothing but love and adoration within her heart.

*

'Sir, can I get you and your guests anything to eat or drink?'

'No, thank you Jane, can you see the guest bedrooms are made up, Father Shaun and Sister Adriana will be staying again.'

'Yes, Sir, anything else?'

'No, Jane, that will be all.'

'Very good, Sir.'

As the maid left the room, the Vicar turned to Shaun and Adriana. 'See, a little discipline and she is happy and content as could be.'

Adriana nodded; the maid did indeed appear to be happy, baring no ill will from her punishment.

'So, what do you make of these murders?' she asked the Vicar.

'A shocking business, shocking. I understand the police are now looking for a single assailant.'

'They no longer believe the High Rip gangs are responsible?'

The Vicar shook his head.

'With the pardon and the reward, not to mention the publicity and the panic caused by the murders, my parishioners are scared, I can tell you. The Police are confident that a member of the gangs would have come forward by now, had they been involved.'

Shaun nodded his head in agreement.

'Any suspects?'

The Vicar shook his head.

'Not really, no. Oh, there are loads of theories. The police have been talking to the local Butchers and Slaughter Men; working on the theory the killer has some idea of the anatomy, human or otherwise. They've brought in a local man, an Inspector Abberline to take charge of the investigation as they suspect the Ripper has a detailed knowledge of the Whitechapel area to be able to come and go unseen.'

A commotion in the hall drew all their attention, and voices filtered through the door.

'Yes, Sir, the Father, and Sister are staying here; they are in the study with the Vicar.'

Moments later a burly man entered the room.

'Fathers, Sister, I am Inspector Chandler, Inspector Spratling said you would be here. He also said you were helpful to him with the Mary Nichols murder and that you might be able to help me sort through the details of another murder.'

'Of course, Inspector, we are only too happy to help. Won't you take a seat?'

The inspector's shoulders straightened noticeably before he shrugged off his coat and, together with his hat, gave both into the care of the Maid.

'A stiff drink, Inspector?' asked the Vicar. 'For medicinal purposes?' he added.

Rising, the Vicar walked to the sideboard, poured a generous measure into a glass, and handed it to the Inspector, whose hand visibly shook.

'Take your time, Inspector.'

'Thank you, Father. I am so angry I am beside myself. Once again, the body was washed before the post mortem was carried out. Who knows what evidence we lost?'

'Who washed it?' asked Adriana, leaning forward.

'Two nurses, acting on instructions from the Workhouse Guardians, apparently.'

Shaun looked at Adriana, an eyebrow raised.

Adriana shook her head slightly.

'Clear instructions were left?' she asked.

'Of course, I made it plain the body was to be left untouched, even placed a PC in charge to ensure it remain so.'

'And yet these women managed to get to the body, strip it and wash it,' Adriana said, more to herself then the Inspector.

'Indeed,' said the Inspector. 'It's going crazy out there since the murder. We only just managed to save a man from being hung by a mob who thought he was the murder.'

'Are you any closer to discovering his identity?' asked the Vicar's wife. 'The murderer I mean.'

'We are getting closer, yes. We discovered a leather apron at the scene. A barmaid says a woman of the description of the victim was drinking at the Ten Bells pub around 5am when she was called outside by a man wearing a skull cap and one Elizabeth Long identified the victim as the same woman she saw talking to a man at 5:30am close to the murder site. Though she didn't see his face she did say he was short, 5ft tall, no more, foreign, wearing a dark overcoat and deerstalker hat. These all point to the assailant being of Jewish descent.'

'So you believe the man in the skull cap is the same man seen talking to the victim close to the murder site as being one and the same?' asked Shaun.

The inspector nodded. 'I do.'

'Was the body mutilated in any way?' asked Adriana.

The Inspector looked at Adriana and then at Shaun. 'Perhaps the ladies should leave the room?'

Shaun nodded and cast a look at Adriana before turning back to the Inspector.

'Sister Adriana was at the Mortuary with the last victim, she can hear what you have to say.'

'Perhaps you should leave, my dear,' said the Vicar. 'You are far too delicate to hear such things.'

The Vicar's wife looked startled before rising, smoothing her skirts, and leaving the room without a word.

'The body was indeed mutilated,' said the Inspector. 'Her throat had been cut like the last one, but not in one clean cut but twice this time, and the placement of the body suggests she put up a struggle. The post mortem revealed her womb had been cut out.'

'Her womb?' asked Adriana.

The inspector nodded. 'Yes, the womb? Would do you make of that?'

'Well, it has connotations with birth of course, and uniquely female; and the victim, was she known in the area?'

'A prostitute you mean? Yes, she would supplement what income she made from her sewing that way,' said the Inspector, looking embarrassed discussing such things with a Nun.

'So all the murder victims have been prostitutes,' said Shaun. 'That could be significant.'

'I think that the bodies were washed despite clear instructions to the contrary is interesting,' said Adriana. 'Someone is confident enough to supersede police instruction in order to remove any physical evidence that might be found,' said Adriana.

The Inspector looked startled.

'I hadn't thought of that. I assumed it was miscommunication, and incompetence.'

'It could be, but let's not dismiss it yet,' Adriana said.

'What news of The Leather Apron?' asked the Vicar.

'The Leather Apron?' asked Shaun.

The Inspector nodded. 'He is our prime suspect at the moment. Real name; John Pizer. He is an unemployed Whitechapel slipper maker who is known in the area as The Leather Apron by the local prostitutes. It was the women of the area that brought his name to our attention, saying he would often extort money from them and beat those who wouldn't or couldn't pay. And he is a Jewish immigrant from Poland.'

'He's in all the papers,' said the Vicar.

The Inspector gave a sigh. 'I fear the papers are stirring up more trouble than they should. Anti Semitism was already rising, the murders have outraged many people, bringing the two factions together. It is a powder keg waiting to explode.'

Shaun nodded. 'It is probably best not to talk to the press.'

'Talk to them? We have no relation with the press I can assure you. They talk to witnesses who are only too happy to share, not only what they saw, but their own thoughts and suppositions too. The reporters make up the rest.'

THE RIPPER NAMED
27ᵗʰ September 1888

Shaun entered the study to find Adriana crying softly, a piece of paper in her hand.

'Where did you come across that?' asked Shaun, taking the letter from her gently.

'I saw Mary's father pass it to you and waited for you to share it with me. When I noticed it sticking out of your pocket, I took it.'

'I see,' said Shaun sternly.

'Don't give me that tone, Shaun. You and I are partners in this venture. You brought me into this madness and yet you keep things from me.'

'I was trying to protect you,' said Shaun, pointing to the handkerchief balled up within her fist.

'A few tears are not going to kill me, and this was important, or at least I think so.'

'Important how?'

'Read it, out loud,' said Adriana.

Shaun frowned, trying to discern her thoughts before holding the letter up and reading aloud.

'"I just write to say you will be glad to know that I am settled in my new place and going all right up to now. My people went out yesterday and have not returned, so I am in charge. It is a grand place inside, with trees..................."'

'You can skip that part and get to the part about them being teetotallers,' interrupted Adriana.

'Ok, hang on,' said Shaun scanning the letter. 'Ok, here we are. "They are teetotallers, and religious so I ought to get on. They are very nice people and I have not too much to do. I hope...."'

'Ok, you can stop there,' said Adriana.

Shaun looked up from the letter.

'I'm not seeing it,' he admitted.

Adriana gave an exaggerated sigh. 'Why would Mary throw away such a position days after writing that letter?'

'Come again?'

Adriana looked at Shaun incomprehensibly before suddenly realising.

'Oh, you don't know.'

Adriana smiled to herself and sat up straight, adjusting her habit, smoothing out the skirt and reaching for her tea.

'Adriana,' Shaun said. Just one word but it made Adriana's heart skip a beat and her skin tingle.

'Ok, ok keep your collar on. Mary left her position suddenly, without a word and according to the Lady of the House, she stole clothing worth over three pounds to boot.'

Shaun sat down, the furrows on his forehead back as he tried to figure out a possible scenario that would fit Mary's behaviour.

'That does seem odd,' he finally said. 'Perhaps the Master of the house made unseemly advances on her? That is not uncommon in these times.'

Adriana nodded. 'Or perhaps the discipline was harsh? She mentions in her letter they are a religious couple.'

Shaun nodded. 'Perhaps.'

'There is something here, I can feel it,' said Adriana.

'Go on,' said Shaun encouragingly.

'I don't have it yet. It's like I have all these pieces floating around but I cannot put them together. I cannot see the picture yet.'

Shaun nodded.

'The Demon will show itself in due course and we will deal with it,' he said confidently. 'I just hope to save a life or two, change the course of history for as many of those unfortunate women as possible.'

Adriana nodded.

'According to history, there were five murders definitely linked to the Ripper, and we have had two of them already.'

Shaun nodded, striding to the window and looking out over the lawn towards the church.

'We're running out of time,' he said.

'You think this Jack the Ripper will strike again soon?' asked the Vicar, walking into the room.

Shaun turned around sharply and cast a look toward Adriana, who returned his look, equally concerned.

How much had the Vicar heard?

'Jack the Ripper?'

'That's what the police are calling him,' said the Vicar, brandishing a piece of paper in his hand.

Adriana and Shaun let out held breaths.

'May I?' asked Shaun, holding out his hand.

'Of course, of course,' said the Vicar, clearly animated, and excited.

'You seem in good spirits?' said Adriana.

'What, spirits? Well I guess so. I say that is awful isn't it? To get excited about such things.'

'For the common man it is understandable, Vicar, but for a man of the cloth?'

Shaun left any further rebuke unsaid as he took a seat and became absorbed by the latest on the "Ripper."

The Vicar flushed red.

'Quite, you are right, but he has named himself,' the Vicar's downcast expression changed back to one of excitement as he sat opposite Adriana, his voice dropping conspiratorially. 'It starts, "Dear Boss,"' he said his voice almost a whisper.

A shiver tingled along Adriana's spine as she leaned in.

'He goes on to taunt the police, mocking their claims that they have caught him.'

The vicar leant back in his seat, his fingers templed beneath his chin.

'He refers, of course, to the Leather Apron, of John Pizer, arrested on the tenth only to be released soon after. Jack called that a joke and had him in fits. He says he is down on whores and "shant quit ripping."'

Adriana looked over at Shaun, who was listening quietly to the Vicar as he shared his thoughts on the letter with evident relish.

'He says he is going to strike again and soon,' said the Vicar, his voice and demeanour taking on a theatrical tone of menace and wickedness. 'He even wrote the letter in blood.'

'And he signed it Jack the Ripper?' asked Adriana.

The Vicar nodded. 'Bold as brass, Jack the Ripper he has called himself. Do you think he is the leader of a High-Rip gang?'

Shaun and Adriana exchanged a startled look.

'I hadn't thought of that,' said Shaun, his eyes losing focus as he reconsidered all that he had learnt of the Ripper Murders.

'What made you think that?' asked Adriana.

'The name of course, The High Rip gangs and Jack the Ripper, perhaps it is a title of some distinction, a leader, as I suggest.'

'Where did you get this?' asked Shaun, holding up the piece of paper.

'I have a parishioner at the News Agency that copied it from the original. Word for word she assures me. She doesn't feel it is being taken seriously, but she was troubled by it and brought it to me.'

'So "The Boss" is the manager of the News Agency, not the Inspector in charge of the case,' said Adriana.

The Vicar looked surprised.

'Yes, that hadn't occurred to me, but you must be right?'

'I think so too,' said Shaun. 'In the first line he writes "I keep on hearing the police have caught me", not "you" have caught me, as he would have written if the letter were addressed to the police.'

'Well, he will find it very difficult to commit more murders now the Vigilance Committee are out in force,' said the Vicar.

'Vigilance Committee?'

The vicar nodded his head.

'The local businessmen have banded together to set up the committee and employ even more Vigilance men to assist the police in catching this man. The streets are well patrolled now.'

Shaun and Adriana exchanged troubled looks, both knowing the Ripper does indeed kill again and soon.

THE DEMON
29th September 1888

Adriana's eyes shot open, and she searched with her eyes and ears for whatever had wakened her.

Seeing nothing but the shadows within the darkness and hearing only the usual sounds of the house settling she flung back her bedclothes and placed her bare feet onto the cold floorboards with an intake of breath.

Something had woken her and trusting her senses she slipped her coat over her nightdress and opened the door just enough to peer into the hallway.

Another "*CRACK*" sounded out, louder this time and she knew instantly someone was moving on the stairs. Her heart pounded as her mind conjured the image of the Ripper slowly creeping up the stairs, long knife shining in the moonlight. The fact there was no moon that night did nothing to assuage her fears, and she waited, her eyes straining for any changes to the pattern of shadows before her.

A minute passed before Adriana placed one foot outside her room.

Then another, her bare feet making no sound.

She paused.

Waiting.

Her breath held, which had been so loud in her ears she feared the Ripper could walk right past her before she knew he was there.

Nothing.

Not a sound.

She walked to the end of the hall and looked over the balcony, down to the stairs and hallway below.

Was that a light?

Had there been a silver of light beneath the door just then?

Adriana closed her eyes, counted to ten, then opened them, but the hallway remained shrouded in darkness.

She placed one foot on the stair and slowly stepped down, pausing, her ears strained for any sound, her heart pounding in her chest as it beat once, twice, before she took another step, pausing again, and then taking another step until she was at the bottom. She wafted her arms as she felt the sweat gather, and a trickle slip down her back.

She moved down the hall.

The door to the basement was ajar; the darkness seemed a little less black or was that just her mind playing tricks on her, was the air moving, a draft, or something else?

Adriana pushed the door open and waited, half expecting something to jump out. The air was moving, warm, hot even and her skin crawled as it caressed her body, seeming to curl around her, seeking her beneath the coat, beneath the nightdress... Her skin goosed at its touch.

Shaking herself of such fancies, she took a step inside the doorway, feeling for the steps with her feet. Slowly she placed her weight down upon the first; letting out a breath as there was no sound to give her away.

Step after step, she eased her way down in the darkness. Each drop of her foot, a breath held tension that had her sweating beneath her clothing.

At the bottom, she used her hands to follow the wall, the blackness being so complete she couldn't tell if the basement was to her left or right or straight ahead.

As she turned, her eyes detected a true light within the darkness, faint, very faint, and red, close to the floor, just a slither really, but welcome nevertheless.

Adriana moved quickly towards it, the warmth welcomed her, beckoned her forward and she went eagerly.

Another door opened before her and she froze, panic screaming in her brain.

The figure within the doorway waved her forward, once, then again, more forcefully, taking a step towards her.

The danger penetrated her fear clouded mind and Adriana breathed and stepped forward, outwardly confident, inwardly terrified.

The woman stood to one side as Adriana walked past, down a tunnel cut into the earth and rock. The slope was gentle at first, then steeper, her step quickening as a result, the woman right behind her, giving her no choice but to descend. But into what?

The narrow tunnel opened out into a cavern lit by firebrands fixed to the walls and a large fire upon a raised dais, over which sat a silver dish. All of this Adriana took in with the first few seconds but what captured and held her attention was the woman standing upon the dais. Her black hair moved as if caught within a storm, her eyes blazed red, reflections from the ruddy glow of the cavern most would assume but not her, she had seen the eyes of a Demon before. The Demon's arms flung out as her words filled the room. However, this was not what occupied Adriana's mind as yet, as another feature was still uppermost, the Demon was completely naked. That in itself would not have troubled her, but the fact the cavern was filled with women, all naked, did. The woman that had followed her down was now removing her own robe, beneath which her naked body was revealed.

With fumbling fingers Adriana undid her coat and shrugged it off, quickly removing her nightdress before it drew attention.

'Men are weak and easy prey to the Devil that walks amongst us,' the Demon intoned.

Adriana moved between the women, moving closer to the dais and the Demon that preached the devilment of whores who sold their virtue for money. Whose diseased ridden bodies stole away the health of husband and son, taking their souls as they took their money and their life.

The women before the Demon swayed and cried out.

'Bring forth the offering,' said the Demon.

Adriana gave a start as she recognised the Demon as the maid to the Vicar and his wife.

The woman walking up behind the Demon caught her attention as her hands dripped blood.

The Nun didn't need to see the offering; it had to be the womb cut from Annie Chapman.

She had found the Ripper.

The organ hissed and popped as it landed amongst the coals.

'Oh, Mistress, take this offering as our promise to rid our streets of the Devil that resides within the whores that steal our husbands and take our sons.'

A hand touched her bottom and Adriana spun around to find a woman suddenly within her arms, her naked body pressed tightly against her own. Someone pressed against her back, trapping her effectively, though there was no menace in their actions. No, this was something far more troubling to her, far more challenging.

All around, the women gathered into groups, often pairs, sometimes in threes, a few in fours or more, all engaged in acts of intimacy and Adriana found herself in the middle of one such group, fingers stroking her, caressing her, entering her.

Her mind a whirl, she twisted her body, seemingly to engage with a chosen woman whilst disengaging from another, working her way towards the edge of the seething mass of bodies, soft cries and moans filling the air.

After what seemed an age, but in truth no more than a couple of minutes; Adriana was close to the tunnel opening and her escape. As the last of the women dropped to the floor, her eyes momentarily met the Demon's, who stood upon the dais watching the orgy below her. With no other choice, Adriana lowered herself, as if succumbing to the hands that reached up.

Women grabbed her, painfully so, as she wriggled herself towards the opening, pulling her breasts free of grasping hands, sliding herself off questing fingers as they sought to hold her amongst them.

Finally free, she raised her head and looked across to the dais to ensure the Demon was not watching. She needn't have worried as the Demon was now engaged with two worshippers satisfying her desires.

Grabbing her nightdress and coat, Adriana moved into the tunnel before quickly getting dressed and hurrying down the passageway, the noises behind her fading quickly as she made her way back to the basement and up the stairs.

Her bare feet barely made a sound on the floorboards as she climbed the stairs quickly, all thoughts of stealth removed in her haste to get to Shaun and share her adventure.

Arriving at his room, she tapped on the door.

'Shaun,' she whispered.

The sound of movement within the room was instantaneous and within moments, the door was open.

'What is it? Are you ok?'

'I am now, can I come in?'

'Of course.'

Shaun moved aside and opened the door as Adriana slipped in.

'I found her, I found the Demon,' she said in a rush.

'What! Where!'

'Ssssshhhh,' said Adriana.

'Down in the basement. She was holding some sort of Service.'

'Demon Worshipers, I wasn't expecting that,' said Shaun, sitting down on the bed.

'I don't think they know,' said Adriana. 'The Demon spoke of prostitutes being devils incarnate and she was doing the Lords work. Though, when she made the offering of Annie's womb, she called out to her Mistress, so I guess they think they are worshipping the Virgin Mary, perhaps?'

'Only, we know different.'

Adriana nodded. 'What do we do? Confront her now?'

Shaun shook his head.

'If her worshippers are devout, they may fight to protect her and we cannot exorcise the Demon whilst fighting off a bunch of women. No, we will wait and watch. It may be the Demon possesses the woman only at times so we need to be vigilant. Would you recognise the woman again if you saw her.?'

Adriana nodded. 'Easily. It's the maid.'

'The maid here?'

Shaun closed his eyes. 'You really do move in mysterious ways sometimes.'

'Pardon?' said Adriana.

'Nothing,' said Shaun.

'Well, it's time I was off to bed,' said Adriana.

'Will you be ok?'

Adriana paused by the door.

'Yes,' she said finally, and opened the door.

Shaun moved to hold it for her.

'God Bless.'

Adriana flashed him a smile and walked across the hall to her own room.

ELISABETH STRIDE
01st October 1888

Adriana watched carefully as the maid walked into the room and around the table filling everyone's cup with piping hot tea. When pouring her tea, Adriana detected a faint smile on the lips of the maid but nothing more, but when she accidentally touched the hand of Shaun Adriana was shocked.

Not by the flash of red in the eyes of the Maid, after all she knew she was a Demon, but by the flash of silvery white within Shaun's.

She knew very little about Father Shaun. Sometimes he spoke as if he had known her before they met, almost a year ago now, when he came to her Convent. Clearly a devote man, his goodness and Faith rolled off him in waves, sometimes so forcefully, it was hard to be around and not be overwhelmed with love and forgiveness. And those eyes, so blue, so gentle and wise, they seem to see everything, understand every emotion and human action and never judge harshly, only compassionately.

Adriana's mind jumped as it focused on one word, just one from all many that were tumbling around her head at that moment; Human.

She had never considered Shaun might not be human, but something more, but that flash of light, was it more than just the reflection of light from the window, coincidental to the Demon red the Maid flashed him?

With a start, she realised those deep blue eyes were fixed on hers and she blushed and dropped her head though she caught the smile that played across his lips and her heart pounded within her chest.

Adriana had reluctantly agreed not to confront the Maid that morning but to wait and watch, a decision she still gnawed away at and her mind teased her with the suspicion that Shaun had wandered around his room that morning in his boxers deliberately to distract her from her intent.

That was another mystery, she had never seen Shaun lift a weight, do a press up, a stomach crunch, or anything, yet he had the body of a Greek god. Huge muscles, chiselled abs, a hard body that was both comforting and thrilling to touch at the same time.

Again, she became conscious she was looking directly into his eyes and this time his smile was broad and she felt herself getting hotter. It was as if he was actually reading her mind, the way his eyes twinkled and his smile was all toothy, and there, on his cheeks, that faint blush of embarrassment she found so endearing.

A knock at the front door drew all their attention and a tingle of anticipation prickled Adriana's skin as a man walked into the room, removing his hat as he did so.

'Detective Halse, it's a pleasure, come in, come in,' welcomed the Vicar. 'Catherine, would you fetch the Detective a cup for some tea and some breakfast please?'

The maid dropped a small curtsey and left whilst the Detective shrugged out of his coat and handed it to the Vicar's wife who took it outside.

'There have been two more murders,' he said, without preamble.

'Two!' exclaimed the Vicar. 'In one night?'

The detective nodded.

'Inspector Chandler said you,' the detective nodded his head in the direction of Father Shaun, 'were staying here and have been helpful with his inquires and that I should update you?'

Shaun nodded. 'Slightly unusual I suppose,' he said hearing the questioning tone in the Detective's voice, 'but the Church is paying particular interest in these murders as you can imagine.'

'Yes, yes of course,' said the Detective. 'I hope it goes without question, what we discuss here stays out of the papers.'

'Of course,' said Shaun. 'It goes without saying.'

'Yes, yes, sorry, but I am a simple man and like things said aloud so there are no misunderstandings.'

'I totally understand, Detective, and I assure you, the Vicar and his wife, myself, and Sister Adriana all are bound by the sanctity of the church and will not discuss anything here with the press.'

Detective Halse nodded as he took a sip of his tea.

'Ummm lovely, nice and hot, just how I like it.'

'You were saying,' pressed the Vicar.

'Just one moment,' said Adriana. 'That will be all Catherine.'

The maid gave a start before dropping a small curtsey and leaving the room, though not before narrowing her eyes at Adriana.

'There were two murders last night,' said Detective Halse.

'*Two?*' said Adriana softly, looking at Shaun. They had spent the night prowling the Rectory to ensure the Maid didn't leave and were confident in their success so to hear there had been not one but *two* murders was shocking news.

The Detective nodded.

'Elizabeth, otherwise known as "Long Liz" Stride, and Catherine Eddows.'

'Were they together?' asked Shaun.

The Detective shook his head.

'No, they appear to be separate murders but both bear the hallmarks of being Ripper murders.'

'What do we know of Elizabeth's movements?' asked Shaun.

'Well, like the others, Liz liked a drink and was seen in the Queen's Head pub at 6:30pm last evening. She returned to her lodging, got ready for a night out, and left again around 7:30pm. She was seen later that night in the arms of a short man in the doorway of the Bricklayer's Arms on Settles Street, hugging and kissing. He had a thick black moustache and sandy eyelashes,' said the Detective looking at his notes.

Adriana cast a look at Shaun but he was lost in thought and didn't return her glance.

'Two men joked about the man being the "Leather Apron" and the couple "went off like a shot", according to the two men, towards Commercial Road despite the fact it was raining hard and their perch in the pub doorway offered them good shelter,' the Detective continued.

'Was she seen again?' asked Adriana.

'Yes, around 11:45 outside 63 Berner Street having a cuddle and a kiss.'

'Same man?'

The Detective shook his head. 'No, whilst about the same height, this man was clean shaven wearing a, sailor like, peaked cap whereas the other man was wearing a Billycock hat.'

Adriana looked at Shaun questioningly.

'Billycock hat?'

'It's like a bowler hat.'

Adriana nodded and looked at the Detective noting his surprise and she silently rebuked herself for blurting out the question.

'What time was the first man seen again?' she asked.

The Detective flipped his notepad back a page.

'About 11pm.'

'So Liz was with one man at 11pm and another at 11:45pm,' she said, more to herself.

The Detective nodded. 'There's more. At 12:30am, PC Smith noticed a man and a woman on Berner Street opposite Dutfield's Yard. This man was young, whereas the others were reported to be middle aged, and he was foreign, with a dark moustache, taller too, about 5ft 7inches and wearing a deerstalker hat.'

'You mentioned Dutfield's Yard. Is that where the body was discovered?'

The Detective gave Shaun an appraising look before saying, 'Indeed. A, young man, Morris Eagle by name, went through the gates into the Yard at 12:35am, after walking his young lady home and saw nothing. But at 1am, just twenty five minutes later, a Mr Louis Diemshutz returned from the market in Westow Hill to the yard and discovered the body.'

'So we can confidently say the murder took place between 12:35am and 1am,' said Adriana.

'Well, Mr Eagle did say the Yard was pitch black, so it's possible he simply missed seeing the body,' said the Detective. 'But we do have a lead. A Mr Schwartz was on Berner Street around 12:45am and saw a man walking ahead of him. This man stopped to talk to a woman in the gateway of the Yard and has identified her as Liz Stride.'

'Wait, so our window just narrowed to between 12:45am and 1am?' said Adriana. 'That's an awfully short window to commit a murder and escape without anyone seeing you, especially as there appears to be quite a lot of people about, considering the hour.'

The Detective nodded. 'It's what is so baffling about this case. How does this man keep getting away unseen, covered in blood no less, and yet not one sighting, nothing? It's like he's a ghost.'

Adriana looked at Shaun. *Could their murder be a ghost not a demon*, she wondered?

Shaun shook his head slightly.

'Do we have anything on his man this Mr Schwartz saw?' he asked the Detective.

The Detective looked at his notebook before replying.

'We do indeed. Mr Schwartz said the man was about 5ft 5inches tall, around 30years of age, dark hair, fair complexion and a small brown moustache. He claims the man grabbed Liz, pulled her, then pushed her down. Liz screamed three times but not very loudly it seems.'

'Did Mr Schwartz intervene?' asked Adriana.

'No, he didn't want to get involved in what he took to be a domestic argument.'

Adriana snorted. 'The whole city is gripped in fear of the Ripper and his first thoughts are of a domestic argument?'

The Detective shrugged. 'That's what he says. He said he crossed the street, and that's when he noticed the second man.'

'The second man?' said the Vicar, making Adriana jump. She had completely forgotten he was there, he had been so quiet.

The Detective looked pleased with the reaction.

'Indeed, a tall chap, nearly six foot, smoking a pipe. It was only as he lit the pipe, that Mr Schwartz noticed him. As he hurried passed both men, the assailant shouted out "Lipski" and the man with the pipe started to follow him. Mr Schwartz run and managed to escape.'

'Are you sure the assailant yelled Lipski, not Lizzie?' asked Shaun.

'I hadn't thought of that,' said Detective Halse. 'I supposed it's possible, but Mr Schwartz used the word "Lipski."'

87

'What does it means? I don't recognise the word, is it a Hebrew word?' asked Adriana.

'No, far as I can tell it doesn't *mean* anything, but it is used as a curse around these parts.'

'A curse?'

'Yes, about a year ago an Israel Lipski was hanged for murdering his landlady. Gruesome business, he poured acid down her throat.'

Adriana gave a shiver. 'And you are sure he was the one who did it?'

The Detective nodded. 'Confessed to it.'

'Could this second man be another passer-by, startled by the curse and took off in the same direction as Mr Schwartz?'

The Detective gave a start. 'I can see why the Inspector wanted you kept in the loop. You have an interesting way of looking at things.'

Shaun nodded his head at the compliment as the Detective made some notes.

'We have our first sighting of the Ripper at last,' said the Vicar.

At the raised eyebrow of the Detective, he continued. 'We know the murder took place between 12:45 and 1am, surely it is too much to suggest that poor Liz was attacked *twice* in those fifteen minute?'

'You make a good point,' said Shaun. 'It is highly unlikely that would be the case. More likely, the man seen pushing Liz to the ground is indeed our murderer.'

'Or woman,' said Adriana.

The Detective looked up at Adriana. 'Come again?'

'The assumption has always been the Ripper is a man. What if he's a she? A woman. That would account for how she escapes without detection and given the 5foot 5inches height, isn't that more likely to be a woman than a man. It is rather short for a man, wouldn't you say?'

The Detective gnawed on his pencil, clearly troubled.

'A woman? A woman,' he said as he made some more notes. 'That would turn the whole investigation on its head, that's for sure.'

'Was anything taken?' said Shaun suddenly. 'Anything from inside the body?'

The Detective shook his head. 'Throat cut, like the others, and possibly strangled beforehand, by the scarf she had around her neck. Curiously no blood splatters though.'

Shaun nodded.

'You said there were two deaths.'

CATHERINE EDDOWS
01st October 1888

'Catherine Eddows,' said the Detective. 'Released from Bishopsgate Police Station at 1am and found dead forty five minutes later, in Mitre Square.'

'Is that far from Dutfield's Yard?' asked Shaun.

'No, not far at all,' said the Detective 'And PC Hutt, the City Goaler who released Catherine, reckons it would have taken her less than ten minutes to reach Mitre Square from the Station.'

'So that puts her murder around 1:15am, leaving the Ripper thirty minutes to carry out his work.'

The Detective shook his head.

'No, not so,' he said looking at his notes. 'PC Watkins passed through the Square at 1:30am and swears it was empty.'

'Could the Ripper have hidden from sight?'

'Not according to Watkins, no. And, five minutes later, three gentlemen saw a man and woman talking together at the junction of Dukes Street and Church Passage.'

'Any description?'

'One of the gentlemen, a Mr Joseph Lawende, is certain the clothing worn by the woman were those worn by Catherine and by the light from a street lamp, reckons the man had the appearance of a sailor, about 5feet 7inches to five feet 9inches tall, fair complexion and a small moustache.'

'That's the same description Mr Schwartz gave of the man attacking Elisabeth Stride,' said Adriana. 'Except for the height, there is a discrepancy there, but height is easily confused.'

The Detective leafed through his notes again.

'With the Stride murder, a William Marshall said he saw a couple standing outside 63 Berner Street at 11:45pm. He mentions the man wearing a small, sailor like, peaked cap, and he says they moved off in the direction of Dutfield's Yard.'

'Can we be sure Catherine was killed by the same person and if so, that that person *is* the Ripper?' asked Adriana.

'I think we can yes,' said the Detective. 'Catherine had her throat cut, same as Liz and the other victims and with Catherine, her stomach was cut and the intestines were pulled out and placed over the right shoulder. A two foot piece was cut off and placed between the body and left arm, which looks deliberate, as was the removal of her right ear.'

'I agree that all seems very deliberate. Was there any blood spray?' asked Shaun.

'No, none.'

Shaun nodded. 'Most likely strangled, like the others.'

Noting the questioning look from the Detective, he went on to say, 'By strangling the victims, the heart stops beating, so when the throat is cut, for example, there is no spurting of blood.'

The Detective wrote furiously in his notebook.

'Where there any other cuts or organs taken?'

The Detective visibly paled as he read from his notes. 'There were cuts across her face, both eyes were cut through, another cut across her nose, so deep it was to the bone and continued down her jaw. The tip of the nose was removed, both cheeks were skinned about an inch and half, the throat was deeply cut on the left side, shallower on the right. The stomach was opened up; the liver had puncture wounds, as if the Ripper had stabbed it. There were cuts on her upper thigh. The womb was cut through and most taken, though the vagina and cervix were untouched.'

Adriana closed her eyes and took a deep breath.

'I'm sorry, sister. I should not have blurted it out like that, but I find it difficult reading. The only blessing is that she was quite dead before the butchery started.'

Adriana nodded. 'That is quite alright, Detective. This killing is more ...' Adriana searched for the words, 'violent, more gruesome than the others. True, the Ripper was interrupted whilst attacking Elisabeth Stride, but Annie Chapman was spared the facial disfigurement. Cutting the face is a personal thing.'

'Annie's face had been beaten,' said the Detective.

Adriana nodded. 'Still, I cannot help but feel there is something more behind these killings then randomness and chance.'

'So, it is likely that the Ripper was interrupted by Schwartz and went searching for another victim,' said the Vicar.

'Really? That would take some nerve wouldn't it?' said Adriana. 'To be so nearly caught whilst committing one murder, to then have the audacity to walk away, unseen, unnoticed, only to commit another, more bloody one, is hard to fathom.'

'I agree. Could Catherine be the Ripper killing and another murderer killed Liz?' asked Shaun.

'It's possible,' said the Detective. 'But what about the description of the killer in both cases? You have to admit the similarities are striking.'

'But I am thinking disguise might be part of the Ripper's methods.'

'Disguise?' said the Detective.

'Yes, take the first man Liz Stride was seen with, short right? Five foot five, which is short for a man. In addition, he had a large dark moustache and sandy eyebrows? To me, they don't naturally go together, so what if it is a fake moustache. The varying heights could be shoes with varying heels, and the different hats and coats, easy enough to change.'

'True, but that would suggest the Ripper is a local, going back and forth to his lodgings to change.'

Adriana nodded thoughtfully. 'And,' she admitted, 'it is unlikely these girls didn't see through the disguise and recognise the person as being the same man or woman?'

'Maybe not,' said the Vicar. 'I have spoken to these ladies of the night and they often describe their, ummmm, gentleman friends, as being faceless, just another man with a.... ummpf, yes well, you get my drift.'

Adriana smiled gently and nodded.

'Do you truly think a woman could be capable of such butchery?' asked the Vicar.

Adriana nodded. 'I do, yes.'

'I am not discounting the woman theory,' said Shaun. It has merit, but going back and forth changing his or her disguise? That, I am not so sure about. We need to look at a map and work out if it were possible given the known movements of the victims, the sightings, and location of the bodies. Though it would explain how the Ripper is able to escape.'

'How so?'

'If she,' he added, with a nod towards Adriana, 'had a bag to put the bloody clothing inside, leaving her in a dress perhaps, then she would be able to walk away, and should anyone see her, they would assume she is a lady of the night, not a gruesome killer.'

'You two have some unusual and challenging ideas. Could I call on you to come down to the station, to the incident room we have set up and share your thoughts with my colleagues?'

'Of course, we would be happy too,' said Shaun standing.

The Vicar rung a bell and the Maid opened the door almost instantaneously.

'Catherine, could you get the coats for the Detective, Father Shaun, and Sister Adriana, they are leaving.'

Catherine gave a small curtsy and left, returning moments later with their coats.

INCIDENT ROOM
01st October 1888

'Well, for me, Kosminski is the Ripper,' said Assistant Commissioner Robert Anderson. 'Schwartz had a good view of the murderer outside Dutfield's Yard and unhesitatingly identified Kosminski as that man, but still refuses to give evidence against him. We have him under surveillance.'

'Why does he refuse? Fear?' asked Adriana.

Anderson shrugged. 'It's not clear and he won't say. I suspect it's because they are both Jews.'

'Really? You think Schwartz would allow the Ripper to go free, out of what, loyalty?'

'No, not exactly. There is a lot of anti-Semitic feeling in Whitechapel, London as a whole, really. I think he fears stirring up more hatred and violence against all Jews if the Ripper turns out to be Jewish.'

'Where does he live?' asked Shaun.

'With his brother, in Whitechapel.'

'So that fits the belief the Ripper lives within Whitechapel or least local to it.'

Robert Anderson nodded.

'What else do we know of Mr Kosminski?' asked Adriana.

'Mad as a hatter,' said Chief Inspector Swanson to general laughter. 'No, seriously, he is. You have talked to him, Father; you'll back me up on that.'

'I have,' said Father Shaun. 'He believes that God has spoken to him and is controlling his actions, that he knows the movements of all mankind. I don't think he has washed in months and shunned the water I had brought in, nor would he accept any food he was offered.'

'And he hates women, especially prostitutes. Like I said, mad as a hatter,' added Swanson.

'Any other theories?' asked Assistant Commissioner Anderson.

'What about Charles Cross?' said Shaun.

'The man who found Mary Nichols?' said Detective Halse.

'Detective, can you remind us of Mr Cross please,' asked the Assistant Commissioner.

'Charles Cross is a local Carman who, whilst on his way to work, along Buck's Row, discovered the body of Mary Nichols. Another man, one Robert Paul, also walking to work along Buck's Row, saw Mr Cross as he approached. Mr Cross called out to him...' the Detective checked his notes, '"come and look over here, there is a woman lying on the pavement."'

'What if Robert Paul interrupted Charles Cross as he murdered Mary Nichols? We know this Ripper is a cool customer, after all, having been discovered murdering Liz Stride, he went on to murder another woman forty-five minutes later,' said Shaun.

'It is intriguing,' said Assistant Commissioner Anderson. 'Charles Cross is by the body at the time of the murder, so we have him at the scene of the crime.'

'According to Cross he was standing in the middle of the road when he realised the "something" he saw was in fact the body of a woman, whereas in Paul's statement he places Cross by the side of the body. His words, "It was dark, and I was hurrying along, when I saw a man standing where the woman was",' said Adriana, looking up from the document she was holding.

'This is something else, though I don't know how significant,' said Detective Halse.

'Go on,' said Swanson.

'Mr Cross gave a false name. Investigation has revealed his real name as one Charles Lechmere.'

'Well, that is suspicious,' said Anderson. 'Why give a false name to the police unless you have something to hide?'

Detective Halse stood up and strode to the large map of Whitechapel.

'He is a local man as he lives here, 22 Doveton Street, Bethnal Green, which is just a few streets from Buck's Row. All the subsequent murders took place between his home and his place of work in Broad Street.'

'Except Liz Stride,' said Adriana, standing up and moving to the map. 'She was killed here, at Dutfield's Yard on Berner Street.'

'But,' said Swanson, 'his mother lives on Cable Street; here. So he may have been on his way home from there.'

'I'm reading from the reports,' said Anderson, shaking some papers in the air, 'the one from Constable Mizen. It says Cross said to him he was wanted in Buck's Row by a policeman, but we know there was no policeman at the scene at that time Cross came across the body,' said Anderson.

'Yes, but Cross's statement says he said, "You are wanted down there." Perhaps Constable Mizen assumed the inference that there was another policeman down on Bucks Row already,' said Adriana, looking up from her copy of the reports.

'At least we know Cross did tell a policeman after all. Early reports suggested he did no such thing,' said Shaun.

Anderson nodded. 'No question, Constable Mizen's statement confirms it. So what do we think? Is Cross our man?'

Swanson shook his head. 'The evidence is circumstantial and based largely on the fact most of the murders were committed along his route to and from work and that he was found by the body of Mary Nichols. No, we need more than that before we can point the finger at Cross.'

'Could the Ripper be a woman,' said Inspector Abberline. 'Or dressed as a woman as Conan Doyle suggests?'

'Sister Adriana had the same thoughts,' said Detective Halse.

'Jill the Ripper? Seriously? I cannot imagine a woman committing these horrendous crimes,' said Swanson.

'Believe me, Chief Inspector, it is entirely possible,' said Adriana.

'Let's step it through,' said Abberline. 'We have been looking for Jack the Ripper as a man, so no one is stopping women as they hurry away from the scene of the crime. Indeed they would have been ushered on by anyone aware that another murder had taken place.'

'What about the surgical knowledge though?' said Halse.

'Good point,' said Swanson.

Silence descended for a moment before Mizen said quietly, 'Midwife?'

'What was that, Constable?'

'Sorry Sir, thinking aloud is all,' said Mizen.

'No, no, you might be on to something, say it again,' urged Anderson.

'Well, what about a midwife? She would have some medical knowledge, especially..... down there,' said Mizen, his face going a deep red.

'Intriguing idea Mizen, well done,' said Swanson.

'Thank you, Sir.'

'A midwife, being a woman, would not be stopped or even her presence noted perhaps during a search for a male murderer, and she would have knowledge of the streets around Whitechapel if she was local *or* assigned to that area,' said Swanson.

'And, no one would think it out of the ordinary if she had blood on her hands or her clothing,' said Anderson.

'And she would have some anatomical knowledge, as Mizen said, especially below the waist,' said Halse, 'and given that the womb was taken, that might point to a midwife too.'

'I think we should instruct our Constables to keep a look out for women in and around the scene of any new murders and go over their notes to see if any mention was made of a midwife seen in the area,' said Anderson.

'Yes, Sir,' said Swanson.

'Let's wrap it up there,' said Anderson, standing up. 'Time for lunch.'

*

'You didn't mention your other theory,' said Shaun, as they walked back to the Rectory.

'The idea of the Ripper being a woman was enough to get their thinking in the right direction, the idea that the Ripper might be more than one woman would have blown their minds.'

Shaun smiled.

'They are good men living in a difficult time.'

'When is time not difficult? Every age has its challenges.'

'That's true.'

'What are we going to do about Catherine?'

'If the Ripper is one person, then she is not our killer, as we know the maid did not leave the Rectory last night, but if you are correct and it is a group of vengeful women, then she could be the ring leader so I think it is time to cut the head off the snake.'

Shaun rolled his shoulders as he spoke, his knuckles cracking as he bulled his hands into tight fists.

'Take a breath, you're starting to glow,' said Adriana.

'What? Oh right.'

Shaun took a breath and visibly dimmed.

'You know Dickens really did depict London well, it is always foggy or wet, the streets are narrow and often dark, despite the street lighting and everything looks.... grim,' said Adriana, looking about her.

Shaun didn't answer; his thoughts were on the battle ahead.

DEMON
01st October 1888

'So you think this child is this Ripper character do you?' said Catherine, standing as cool as you like in the study, glaring at Adriana.

'I saw you down in the Cavern, burning Annie Chapman's womb,' said Adriana.

The Demon's eyes glowed red.

'You have no idea what you truly saw, Sister! So you were amongst my brethren were you? With the women that worship me? Did you stay long, did you enjoy yourself?'

'They do not know *you*, Demon. You have drawn them in with your deceit and lies, as is your way.'

Catherine laughed.

'Drawn them in? They were meeting before I arrived. I just gave them a purpose, a focus for their anger and frustration.'

'Men,' said Adriana.

'Yes, at first, but their anger is harder to turn towards them than I suspected. The women that stole their affections; that's who they blame for their husbands and sons' waywardness.'

Catherine turned her eyes to Shaun.

'Do you think this child is the Ripper?'

Her hands ran over her body, caresses the curves, cupping the breasts in obvious delight.

'No, I don't. We know you did not leave here last night and there was another murder. I think you were drawn to this area by the evil that pervades it,' said Shaun, 'but it is time you were gone from this body.'

'You know I'm not Her right?'

'I do,' said Shaun.

'And does she know who you really are?' asked Catherine, nodding towards Adriana.

'She does; some at least; though she doesn't remember it.'

'Curious,' said Catherine, looking at Adriana intently. 'She is familiar, but I cannot quite place it.'

'It doesn't matter; it's you we are here for.'

'Naturally. It has been entertaining stirring up the women's passions, though honestly, they were simmering away when I got here, really took all the fun out of it, and the evil of the Ripper? I cannot even claim credit for that, it has been.....' the Demon sought for the right word, 'disappointing. And the weather..........'

'It will be nice and warm where you're going.'

Catherine looked at Shaun speculatively. 'You think you are strong enough to defeat Her?'

Shaun rolled his shoulders. 'I am looking forward to finding out.'

Catherine laughed. Not a genteel feminine laugh but a guttural bark that sounded at odds with the beautiful woman it came from.

'Typical man, all brawn, and no brains. You may have got rid of Andhaka, but there are three more of us to stand with Her, you think you can take us all?'

Shaun pulled a bible from his pocket.

The smile that spread across Catherine's face was full of evil glee.

'I'm supposed to say something like, "I hate to spoil your moment, Father", but that would be a lie.'

Catherine's eyes suddenly rolled upwards into her head until they showed only the whites, moments before her knees buckled and she fell.

Shaun shot forward, catching her before she hit the floor and gently lowered her.

Adriana looked up at the blackness that gathered, suspended above them and the figure within, the Demon, naked, muscled, its dark wings spread wide, the black smoke emanating from its form, its sharp-toothed mouth open with mocking laughter.

'BEGONE IN THE NAME OF THE FATHER,' Adriana intoned, stepping forward.

'As you command,' said the Demon. The black smoke swirled around her body getting thicker, hiding her form until it disappeared.

Adriana peered into the smoke as it slowly cleared, only to reveal the Demon had vanished.

Catherine gave a gasp as air rushed into her lungs, her eyes snapped open, and she screamed.

A scream that sent shivers down Adriana's spine.

*

'So the Ripper is still out there?' said Adriana.

Shaun nodded. 'The Demon's presence increased the evil hereabouts; it's possible with its departure the Ripper will stop.'

'Let us hope so.'

MURDER!
3rd October 1888

'Father, Sister, thank you for coming.'

'Of course, Chief Inspector, we are happy to help.'

'This is Doctor Thomas Bond. We have another body.'

Shaun looked at Adriana.

'Doctor Bond, could you tell the Father about the latest victim?'

'Of course. The body was found in the basement vault of the new police buildings. It was wrapped in cloth, and laid there for at least three days, more I think, as the wall behind it was stained black. I say body, all there was, was the torso. The head had been removed, the legs from the pelvis on down, the arms as well. The trunk was decomposed which made investigating a challenge but I couldn't detect any wounds. I would place the time of death somewhere between six weeks to two months ago.'

'August then?' said Swanson.

'Aye, August,' said Bond.

'Can you add anything else?' asked Shaun.

'Well, I would estimate her height to be five foot eight, so tall for a woman, healthy, well fed, and the arm, that was later brought to me, fitted perfectly and showed this lady to be of means, as there were no signs of manual labour apparent on the hands.'

'The work of the Ripper?' asked Swanson.

Bond shrugged. 'That is not for me to say. The dismemberment is not in keeping with the other murders. Those ladies kept their limbs, though they had other parts removed. So it is possible.'

'For the sake of the press we will say *not* the Ripper,' said Swanson. 'Is that understood?'

'Yes, Chief Inspector,' said the Doctor.

'Of course, Chief Inspector,' said Shaun, with a bow of his head. 'Chief Inspector have there been other murders?'

'Murders? Of course, but none that we have attributed to the Ripper.'

'Perhaps we should explore some of the more recent ones, say, going back a year.'

'If you think it would help, Father, I will gather the others.'

It might be useful,' said Shaun.

*

'The Father here thought it might be useful to take a look at some of the murders that have taken place going back about a year, to see if there are any Ripper connections.'

'Yes, Sir,' said Inspector Spratling. 'A year you say, so to the night of the great storm.'

'Great storm?' said Adriana.

'Oh my, yes, Sister, it was truly something. The thunder shook the heavens and the lightning lit the sky.'

'And the rain?' asked Adriana.

'That was the odd thing, Sister, there was none. Have you ever heard of the like?'

'Actually, I have,' said the Sister.

'The murders, Inspector?' urged Shaun.

'Well, just after the Storm, Boxing Night it was, we found a murdered woman in the alleys of Commercial Street. She was on her way home, close to Mitre Square.'

'So location wise, it fits with the Ripper killings,' said Anderson.

'Indeed, Sir,' said Inspector Abberline, 'but that is pretty much where the investigation ends. We never identified her, or got any further in finding her killer.'

'There was talk of mutilation,' said Detective Halse, 'but the file went missing and the body was buried who knows where.'

'Well that is not very satisfactory, sloppy in fact, very sloppy. I'm not happy, Detective but let's press on,' said Anderson.

'Sir,' said Halse. 'The next that I think is worth a mention is Annie Millwood. Back in February, she actually survived an attack that bare similarities with the Ripper killings as she sustained multiple stab wounds to her legs and lower torso, similar to those of Martha Tabram. Not as many as Martha mind, though to this day we have not counted her murder as a Ripper attack, believing she was a victim of a High Rip gang member.'

'But she saw her attacker, so we have an eye witness,' said Abberline. 'We should bring her in immediately.'

'Unfortunately Sir, she died of natural causes at the end of March.'

'Natural causes?' said Adriana.

'Yes, Sister, so was the conclusion of her inquest.'

'Did she say anything about her attacker?' asked Shaun.

'Only that is was a man, a stranger, and he used a clasp knife.'

'So, we have two unsolved crimes with tangible links to our Ripper. The first was mutilated, the second stabbed a number of times, in her legs and lower abdomen, which shares commonalities with all our Ripper killings, in particular Martha Tabram. Any more?'

'Yes, Sir, I am afraid so,' said Halse. 'Though we have not concluded any possible link to the Ripper Murders, there was an attack on one Ada Wilson on the 28th March. The report states a short man, 5ft foot six inches, red of face, "sunburned," she said, with a fair moustache, attacked her with a knife, in her home. Her throat was stabbed several times when she refused to hand over her money. He thought her dead when he left her, and was nearly caught by neighbours but managed to escape. Ada lived to tell her tale.'

'Well, that puts paid to my idea of the Ripper being a woman,' said Adriana. 'This man bears a striking resemblance to the man described at the scene of the other murders, such as Elisabeth Stride. Jack is a short man with a fair haired moustache.'

'You believe the man who attacked Ada is the same man who killed and mutilated the other women, Mary, Annie, Elisabeth, and Catherine?' said Spratling.

'It's certainly possible Inspector, given the description,' said Adriana. 'Or a separate attacker, one who went on to attack Martha in August. Whilst moustaches are not rare, for a short man with a moustache to be connected to the attacks *and* the murders that have occurred, cannot be a coincidence, surely.'

'Detective, do we have any more cases to drawn upon,' said Shaun. 'Perhaps we are closer to our Jack than ever before.'

The tension in the room was palpable as the Detective looked through several case files before pulling out another.

'Emma Smith died of injuries sustained when she was beaten, raped, and assaulted on her way home in the early hours of the morning. She lived long enough to say her attackers were four young men, one of whom jabbed something large and blunt between her legs. She died of complications that resulted from the attack.'

'So, another murder by one of these so called High Rip gangs,' said Abberline.

'Yes, Inspector that was the conclusion of the investigation.'

'Detective, I want any member of these gangs, found with a weapon matching the description of that which was used on these two poor unfortunate women, arrested at once. The charge, carrying an offensive weapon, is that clear.'

'Yes, Sir.'

'The Vicar had an interesting thought,' said Shaun. 'That the self titled Ripper, might be part of, or head up, one of these gangs. A thought concluded by the association of the names, the High Rip gang, and the Ripper. An honorary title bestowed on their leader perhaps?'

'Or some kind of initiation,' said Adriana suddenly. 'The name Ripper being that of initiate or new joiner.'

'That is a troubling thought,' said Anderson, 'as it would suggest these murders will never stop.'

'But it does give reason to why the Ripper, after being discovered killing Elisabeth Stride, went onto to kill Catherine Eddows. Perhaps, as part of the initiation, the Ripper has to bring back a trophy, as proof of his deed.'

'Or perhaps there were two initiates that night,' said Halse.

'One peculiar aspect to this case is Fingers Freddy. Now he was Elisabeth's protector, and boasted that he knew who the Ripper was. He's not been seen or heard of since Emma's death.'

'Do you think he's been killed too?' asked Adriana.

Halse nodded. 'I do. I think the Ripper killed him or had him killed. The peculiar thing about it is; he said, before he disappeared, that the Ripper was a woman.'

'So we are back, full circle, to being no closer to identifying our Ripper after all,' said Anderson.

'I wouldn't say that, Assistant Commissioner,' said Shaun. 'The very fact every case throws up, not only something new but also contradictory to the direction the investigation is taking could be the very thing that explains everything.'

'Come again?' said Halse.

'Yes, you have lost me to, Father,' said Spratling.

'Well, we have our short man, with the moustache, seen at both the scenes of the crime for Ade Wilsons and Elisabeth Stride, yet Emma was attacked, most likely, by the High Rip Gang, Annie Chapman and Catherine Eddows both had their wombs removed. Whether it is significant only time will tell but Catherine's face was heavily disfigured, with cuts to her eyes, nose, cheeks, and jaw. The only common thread amongst our victims is that they were all prostitutes.'

'And?' said Anderson, 'how does any of that further our investigation?'

'Well,' said Shaun. 'I propose that not all of these killings are by the same person. That either we have more than one Ripper, but working together, perhaps members of the same gang, or we have another murderer taking advantage of the Ripper murders, killing at will, happy to let Jack take the blame.'

Silence descended as everyone considered this latest proposal.

'It doesn't get us any closer to the Ripper,' said Anderson, 'but it is an intriguing thought. Whether this man with the moustache could be our Ripper, or the other murderer, makes no difference. We have a description to go on. Halse, get that circulated amongst the men immediately, *but* no mention that we might have two killers at large; the city is in a panic enough. Let's just hope we can apprehend him before he kills again.'

MARY KELLY
9th November 1888

'Gentleman, and Lady,' Abberline gave a nod towards Adriana, 'we having another murder. A Mary Kelly was discovered this morning, murdered in her bed. Inspector Dew, why don't you bring us up to speed?'

'Yes, Sir. Inspector Beck and I were in the station when Mr Bowyer arrived. He was so frightened we couldn't understand a word he was saying. Just a few words made sense, "another one" he said, "Jack the Ripper" next and then he choked out the word "awful." We sat him down, gave him some water. Calmer he added that Jack McCarthy had sent him.'

'Jack McCarthy?' said Shaun.

'Runs the shop and Miller Court lodgings were Mary Kelly rented a room these last eight months,' said Dew.

'Go on,' said Abberline.

'When I got to Miller's Court... I'm sorry,' said Dew swallowing. 'I still get nauseous when I think about it, the horror..............'

'It's ok. Take your time,' said Adriana, reaching out her hand and placing it on Dew's.

Dew nodded, took a deep breath then said in a rush........

'Mary Kelly's body was on the bed. She was facing the window, her eyes wide open filled with the terror of her ordeal. Her lover Barnet could only identify her by her eyes, her face...' Dew's voice broke. 'Her face was savaged to the point she is unrecognisable.'

'Ok, Inspector, I won't ask you to describe any more, we get the picture, it's like the others,' said Swanson.

'No, no, that's the point, it's not like the others; this was vicious, barbaric. Mary was cut to pieces. There was blood everywhere.'

'This boyfriend; a suspect?' asked Abberline.

'Barnet? He says he was with Mary for about an hour last night leaving around 7:45pm, during which time a Lizzie Albrook turned up, but that is not the strangest thing,' said Dew.

'Oh?' said Swanson.

'We talked to a Mrs Maxwell who swears she saw Mary Kelly this morning after 8am and again after 9am talking to someone, a man, outside the Britannia public house.'

'Perhaps she was mistaken about the time? Or perhaps it was someone that looked like Mary?' suggested Adriana.

Dew shook his head. 'I thought so too, but Mrs Maxwell's husband returns home at 8am each morning, that's how she remembers the time so accurately for the first sighting and she describes the clothing; dark shirt, velvet bodice and a maroon shawl. The shawl particularly caught her eye, as it is something she remembers Mary having worn before. She did mention that Kelly looked quite unwell when she first saw her.'

'Perhaps pale from having committed such an atrocious killing,' said Adriana.

'What do you mean?' said Abberline.

'Well, consider this. After committed her foul deeds, the Ripper takes Kelly's shawl so if anyone saw her they would mistake her for her victim. Maybe all the clothes were Kelly's, the Ripper's own clothing being covered in blood.'

Abberline looked thoughtful. 'You know, I think you could be on to something there. I will discuss this seriously with Dr Thomas Dutton as I feel it has merit.'

'Have you noticed the dates,' said Shaun, picking up a piece of chalk.

Mary Nichols died on Friday 31st August.

Annie Chapman Saturday 8th September

Elisabeth Stride and Catharine Eddow, Sunday 30th September

And Mary Kelly this morning, Friday 9th November.

All committed between Friday and Sunday, could be nothing or could be significant.'

Shaun placed the chalk down and returned to his spot, sitting on the edge of the desk, arms folded.

'Cattle boats arrive Thursdays and leave Mondays,' said Anderson. 'Not sure if that's significant, but I thought it was worth mentioning.'

'Ties in with the idea the Ripper is a sailor,' said Anderson.

'Some of the Detectives are working on the theory the Elisabeth Stride murder was not a Ripper killing,' said Inspector Dew.

'Reason?' asked Abberline.

'Her throat was cut from left to right whereas the other four were cut right to left.'

'That is interesting,' said Anderson, 'but the descriptions of the men both Elisabeth and Catherine were seen with are so similar, it's hard to discount it.'

Abberline stood and strode around the room.

'This is maddening. Every time we're onto something, another theory presents itself, and then another and another.'

'There is one more thing, something discovered during the post mortem,' said Dew.

'Yes, what is it?' asked Swanson.

'Mary was three months pregnant.'

Silence.

No one moved; no one spoke as everyone absorbed this latest piece of information, the sadness pervading the room was tangible.

'How? How is he getting away with this?' said Swanson. 'The whole city, is terrified, the whole country is watching. Women, especially prostitutes, are saying we are not doing enough to keep them safe despite having every available bobby on the streets, not to mention the Vigilants. How is this killer walking up to these women, strangling them, and then mutilating them and no one hears a thing?'

'They are all prostitutes, selling their bodies for the money needed to doss down somewhere for the night. Desperate, they are taking chances others wouldn't,' said Dew. 'We know at least two of the victims were turned away from lodgings for not having their doss money, before they were killed.'

'And they all like a drink,' said Adriana. 'So either their senses are dulled or perhaps someone is slipping them something to make them more manageable?'

'If the Ripper is a woman, other women would be less guarded, allowing her to get close enough to murder them,' said Abberline.

'And if she was a midwife, any blood on her clothing and hands are easily explained,' said Swanson, 'and she would have tonics to dull the pain and the like, to slip into her victims drink, as the Sister suggests.'

'And, perhaps Mary was seeking an abortion which would explain why she was killed in her room whereas the others were killed on the streets.'

'But why the barbarity of Mary's killing,' said Dr Thomas Bond. 'It was vicious but not mindless, it was in rage, but has a detached coldness about it too.'

'Explain?' said Anderson.

'Well, the face, all but destroyed, suggests rage, anger, but personal like. Then the killer sets about his butchery, removing the breasts, cutting the arms, opening the abdomen, placing these bits deliberately, such as the womb, kidneys and one breast under Mary's head, whilst the other breast by her foot, intestines removed and placed to her right, spleen to her left, liver between her feet. This suggests calmness, a cold, methodical evisceration. Ritual perhaps?'

'Which, for me, doesn't really marry with the Ripper being a woman,' said Swanson.

'Perhaps a man dressed as a woman?' said Shaun. 'We have already considered the possibility of disguise. What if our man could pass for a woman? He's short, five feet five inches or so, fair complexion, it's dark, foggy, or raining during the murders, furthering the effectiveness of a disguise?'

'Another theory as good as any other,' said Anderson, throwing down his pencil.

'Is there any religious iconography going on with the placement of the organs?' asked Abberline.

Shaun shook his head.

'Not that I am aware of, no. Nor Demonology either, the placement, whilst deliberate does seem to be personal to the murder.'

'One other thing that just came to mind,' said Dew.

'Another, one more thing?' said Swanson smiling.

'Yes, sir, sorry, sir, I just remembered this from Constable Hutt, the city gaoler who released Catherine Eddows in the early hours of the morning, he said she gave *her* name as Mary Kelly.'

THEORY
9th November 1888

'Well, we finally have something,' said Shaun as they stepped out onto the street.

'Really? I am at a loss,' admitted Adriana.

'It was your suggestions that has allowed me to draw my conclusions,' said Shaun.

'Come on then, don't keep me in suspense.'

Shaun looked up and down the street to make sure there was no one close enough to hear.

'There is more than one murderer, I'm sure of it. That last piece of information clinched it.'

'About Catherine giving a false name?'

'Yes, not the fact she gave a fake name but the name she chose, Mary Kelly.'

'The same name as the latest victim,' said Adriana, beginning to follow Shaun's line of thought, 'and the first victim, if we discount Emma Smith and Martha Tabram, was Mary Ann Nichols.'

'Exactly, three Marys. Can that be a coincidence? And you said it yourself, the disfigurement of their faces is personal, vengeful and both Catherine and Mary's faces were heavily mutilated.'

'But what about Mary Ann Nichols, she was not so disfigured?'

'But what if she *was* the first victim; and Charles Cross disturbed the Ripper before she could complete her murder, that could account for why the face was not as viciously attacked, though there were some cuts and bruising, or the womb taken. Remember, there were cuts across her stomach, which fits with the narrow time line between the act and Cross finding the body? What if our murderer is seeking Mary for a personal slight, only she, and I think it is a she, doesn't know this woman, only her first name and that she is a prostitute, a pregnant prostitute?'

'Which is why the Ripper is cutting out the wombs,' said Adriana. 'The investigation revealed that Mary Ann Nichols was well liked and her father reported at the inquest he was unaware she had any enemies. So not having another motive for her murder, mistaken identity fits.'

'And poor old Catherine, gave up a false name to the police, not realising she also gave herself a death sentence.'

Adriana nodded. 'Emma Smith was attacked and killed by the High Rip Gangs. Martha Tabram was attacked and killed, I believe, by her Guardsman client, given the number of stab wounds, 39 in all, all but one with a simple pen knife, the other possibly by a bayonet, this suggests to me the first wound was inflicted by a bayonet, and the others inflicted to hide that fact. A short man with a fair moustache attacked both Ada Wilson and Elisabeth Stride. That leaves us with Annie Chapman and the torso found in the basement of the new police buildings.'

'We can discount the torso; as limb dismemberment is not part of the Ripper's MO, Annie Chapman however... give me a moment,' said Shaun.

'Actually, I think I can answer my own question,' said Adriana. 'Remember, Elisabeth Long said she saw a man and a woman around 5:30am talking loudly, the man being short, about five foot, Elisabeth guessed, foreign and with a dark complexion. No mention of a moustache but that could fit the knife wielding attacker of Ada and Liz Stride.'

'But she had her womb taken, whereas Mary Nichols did not,' said Shaun.

'Umnmm, yes that does present a wrinkle in the theory, and Annie was the first of the victims associated with the

Ripper to have her womb removed, which ties in with the theory of the pregnancy but not the names. Did she use the name Mary at all?'

'No, and she was ill, dying, according to the Coroner. He didn't say it but, given the Coroner's report, I say she had syphilis.'

'And the intestines were placed over one shoulder, which is a characteristic of the other murders, so we have to include Annie in with the Ripper murders though why, we don't know as yet,' said Adriana.

'I agree,' said Shaun. 'So the Ripper is on the hook for Annie Chapman, Mary Kelly, Mary Nichols and Catherine Eddows, but not Elisabeth Stride. That one always rankled, as it stretches the imagination that our Ripper killed one woman and then run off and killed another, taking more time with the second than the first, and that was the only night the Ripper killed twice, if he or she did both.'

'Isn't that the boy we saw at the site of Emma Smith?'

'It is,' said Shaun. 'It's time we had a word with our young friend.'

Moving quickly, they crossed the street, heading in the same direction as the boy but on the other side of the road. Feigning no interest, they walked along and once they were level with the boy, Shaun darted across the road and grabbed the boy before he could run off.

A man sitting on a stool outside a warehouse stood up, but Father Shaun pulled his coat open, displaying his collar, which satisfied the man and he sat back down.

'Calm down,' said Shaun, holding the boy easily as he squirmed and twisted.

'Let me go, Mister, I ain't done noffink.'

'I think you want to talk to us, no?'

Adriana moved a little closer and placed her hand upon the boy's.

'We are not going to hurt you, we just want to talk.'

Her soft voice and touch calmed the boy, and he looked at her, not at Shaun, who still held him by the scruff of his collar.

'I don't mean no 'arm, miss, honest I don't, but it ain't natural it ain't.'

'What isn't? What isn't natural?'

'All the blood see, all over the insides. I have to cleans it I do, and it has bits in it, flesh like. I swears I saw an ear I did. And my Mistress, she's changed she has. Used to be so nice, gives me things.'

The boy held up a comb that had a couple of teeth missing. Something a Mistress of means would throw out, but to a boy with nothing, it would be a treasure.

'But not now?'

'Not for a long time. Not since her 'usband and boy died. Not since then. Changed she has. Mean she can be, Her *and* her maid. She's changed an all.'

'What did her husband and son die of, do you know?'

The boy nodded. 'The pox, they died of the pox. Got it from the whores they did. One came to visit she did, but the maid sent her packing.'

'What is the name of your Mistress?'

'You won't say I said?'

'No, we won't say you said,' said Adriana.

'Mrs Canonical. She lives up in the big ouse.'

Shaun looked at Adriana.

'Ok, run along,' said Adriana, pressing a penny into his hand.

'Thank you, miss,' said the boy, tugging his hair and ran off.

'Didn't the Vicar say he was going up to visit Mrs Canonical this afternoon?' said Shaun. 'Something about her usual Vicar going missing. No one has seen or heard from him since the 1st October?'

The pair of them hurried back to the Rectory.

'So you think Mrs Canonical is our Ripper?'

'I do, yes. It all fits. Husband and son lost to syphilis, caught from a prostitute called Mary. One who came calling, no doubt to reveal she was carrying their child. It explains the removal of the womb, the rage in the attacks, the facial mutilation; that is such a personal thing. Mrs Canonical was looking for Mary Kelly, to kill her. The others were collateral damage.'

'Or perhaps a clever plan, with so many murders, one stops looking for a reason why, and that is the only clue that points back to Mrs Canonical.'

'Good point,' said Shaun. 'We need to get to her before he does.'

MRS CANONICAL
1ˢᵗ October 1888

'Vicar, how lovely, come on in.'

'Mrs Canonical, lovely to see you again, how are you keeping? Well, I trust?'

'Fine, fine, Vicar, you know me, not one to complain. Here let me take your coat and hat'.

'True true, Mrs Canonical. You have suffered so much, lost so much but never once have I heard you complain.'

'Let's just put this on the coat hook, there, and the hat can sit just so, on top. There, all done. What were you saying, Vicar? I swear I am going quite deaf.'

'I was saying about your loss, Mrs Canonical, the loss of your husband and son.'

'Yes, yes quite, no need to shout, Vicar, I'm not deaf you know. Come, let's go into the parlour, forgive the mess.'

'Come come, Mrs Canonical, you are being too modest, never have I seen a house so clean, so ordered, everything in its place, a place for everything.'

'You are too kind. Please have a seat, Vicar. I'll just go and fetch the tea. Sit by the fire if you feel cold. My old bones feel the cold these days.'

'Come now, Mrs Canonical, you are a woman still in her prime, if I may be so bold.'

'Ha ha, please, Vicar you flatter me so. I'm 48 as you well know, a good age for a woman in these times.'

'Indeed. Here let me help you with that, Mrs Canonical.'

'Oh thank you, Vicar, the tray seems heavier these days.'

'Did you hear there was another murder in town last night?'

'Just the one?'

'Two! Can you believe it? An Elisabeth Stride and a Catherine Eddows. The city is in uproar.'

'Oh, Vicar, I don't follow such things, I am just a woman you know, spending my day reading and sewing and receiving guests of course. Elisabeth and Catherine you say...?'

'Yes, yes of course, I should not talk about such distasteful things. They say he must be a surgeon.'

'Who's that, dear?'

'The Ripper, they say he must be a surgeon, like your husband.'

'A surgeon, yes, my husband was a great surgeon, Vicar, a great surgeon.'

'I expect you miss him greatly, he died last March if I remember correctly.'

'Indeed you do and indeed I do. I miss the family time, him, my son, and me, down in the basement working on the cadavers.'

'I'm sorry, did I miss hear you, Mrs Canonical? Did you say you used to work on cadavers?'

'Oh no, dear me, where ever did you get an idea like that, oh you make me laugh, oh my. Now you have tears in my eyes, oh my.'

'Of course, I must have misheard, most amusing.'

'How I would like to cut them to pieces whilst they are still awake. Oh, Vicar, you have spilt your tea, please be careful, so hard to get out of the rugs you know. I was saying would you like me to cut you a piece of cake?'

'Oh cut a piece of cake, oh yes, oh yes, I thought you said..., no never mind, oh my.'

'I am very lucky in a way, Vicar,'

'Lucky, Mrs Canonical, in what way?'

'Well, if they had not passed the Married Woman's Property Act last year, I would have lost my house and become a ward of my brother. At least now I get to keep my house and my horses.'

'Yes, I saw two of those outside with your carriage. Magnificent beasts, they pawed the ground and snorted most impressively as I walked up. Are you going out later?'

'Going out, where would I go, Vicar? I have nowhere to go. I just came back from killing a whore. I have a boy here that takes care of the horses. Oh dear, are you ok, Vicar? Did the cake go down the wrong hole, should I pat you on the back do you think?'

'No, no that is quite, em em, quite all right. You were saying?'

'I was saying I have nowhere to go, I am feeling quite the bore.'

'No, not at all, Mrs Canonical, though I am sure since the tragic loss of your son most recently it must be very quiet around here? He died in August of this year did he not? I am sure you miss them both.'

'Indeed, Vicar, indeed, most sorely. I do miss breakfast the most, with my husband and son; he used to say "nothing like a good whoring before breakfast".'

'I am sorry, Mrs Canonical, A good whoring?'

'Why, Vicar, please. I am a lady of good breeding; please do not offend my ears with such vulgarities. If you must speak of *those women,* please use a more genteel term. I said herring; we used to enjoy a good herring for breakfast. Really!'

'My sincerest apologies, Mrs Canonical, please forgive me, it's just both husband and son died of syphilis wasn't it?'

'Yes, indeed, Vicar, My husband and son both frequented the theatre in London, Whitechapel I believe, and it was not unusual they would enjoy the company of other women whilst there, one in particular, I understand, caught both their fancy.'

'Yes quite, not in keeping with the Scriptures, Mrs Canonical but a sign of the times, a sign of the times.'

'Indeed, Vicar, perhaps if you had preached a little more about a man's duty and less about a woman's they might not have strayed so far.'

'Uh hum, quite, yes, that is a lovely vase, Mrs Canonical, a family heirloom?' said the Vicar, seeking to change the subject. The visit was proving most disturbing. 'It looks lovely. Interesting shape and those snowdrops around the side, and that single ruby red bead just hanging off the rim is quite lovely. Such purity, such perfection, quite like yourself, if I may say so?'

'Oh, please, Vicar you flatter me so, I have nothing to do with purity let me tell you. I enjoyed ripping out their parts.'

'I beg your pardon?'

'I was saying, Vicar; you sound like you are tipping your hat at my heart,'

'Well, Mrs Canonical, may I call you, Jacqueline? Would that be so bad? I have always thought highly of you, perhaps you would do me the honour of dining with me one evening.'

'Oh why of course, Vicar, I would love that. And please, feel free to call me Jacqueline, or simply Jack.'

'Jack? That would be unusual would it not?'

'Oh, Vicar, really! You cannot call me Jack. Jacqueline, Jacqueline will do, why are you being so familiar? You, a man of the cloth.'

'Of course, my apologies, I am quite mishearing you today.'

'That is quite all right, Vicar, Come I will see you out, I have my bloody knife to clean.'

'Clean? ah, sorry, what was that?'

'I was saying, Vicar, I am still a housewife, and I need to clean.'

'Oh yes, yes of course, but your house looks so perfect as always.'

'Why thank you, vicar that means a lot to an old lady, I look forward to cleaning you out. Don't forget your coat and hat.'

'Why thank you, Jacqueline. My, that is a lovely leather coat, Jacqueline, is it yours?'

'Oh my no; that was my late husbands, God rest his soul.'

'Oh, just that it looks wet, see there is a puddle on the floor.'

'Yes, yes quite; that will be from the blood.'

'Blood, Mrs Canonical? Was someone hurt?'

'Hurt, Vicar, why would someone be hurt, it was just a flood?'

'Oh f f f f flood, my,my,my hearing these days, perhaps I'm the one going deaf,' stuttered the Vicar

'Perhaps Vicar, perhaps. Catherine Eddows you say?'

'Catherine Eddows, Jacqueline?'

'You said the Ripper killed a girl called Catherine Eddows last night? Are you sure that was her name?'

'Why yes, quite certain. I must take my leave, Jacqueline. Again I am sorry for your losses; just know they are in heaven now.'

'That's a crock of shit, Vicar.'

'What? Mrs Canonical, Jacqueline, there is no need...'

'A flock of sheep, Vicar, over there in the fields, aren't they lovely?'

'Why, yes, quite lovely. Well, goodbye, Jacqueline, I will send a note about that dinner.'

'Are you feeling well, Vicar?'

'No, No, I feel quite of odd,' said the Vicar.

'That will be the tea Vicar, come this way. Quickly if you would; before you pass out.'

*

'Arrh good, Vicar, you are awake, excellent. I'm just cleaning my knives, I won't be a moment, be right with you. A tidy house, tidy mind is what I always say. Each knife has its own place on the tray.'

"Blessed is the man who walks not in the counsel of the wicked."

'Quite right, Vicar. Straighten up there Mr Bone Saw we will be needing you today.'

"A woman must quietly receive instruction with entire submissiveness."

'Yes, Vicar and I received my instruction well. See, these knives have become like family to me, since I lost my own family to that godless whore. Each has its own character you know. Mr Bone Saw is dogged and determined. Mr Hammer is very forceful, bit heavy handed sometimes, and Miss Scalpel is sharp, gets to the heart of the matter, no messing. They all share a wicked sense of humour you know, they'll cut you to the quick.'

'Cut you to the quick, no, nothing? Tough crowd.'

"I do not allow a woman to teach or exercise authority over a man but to remain quiet."

'Yes, Vicar, I know. Ropes not to tight, the gag not to uncomfortable, the chair not to hard?'

'All necessary of course, once the cutting starts.'

'Then it can be all wriggles and writhing and screaming. The screaming is enough to give you a headache I can tell you. So it works best with ropes and stuff. Normally I would strangle you, after I slipped a little something into your drink but not this time I think, the gag will suffice, no one but my maid to hear, and she will be joining us shortly.'

"Husbands love your wives, as Christ loved the church and gave himself up for her."

'I loved my husband, Vicar but do you think he loved me as he should? If so, why was he with that disgusting diseased woman? There now, everything in its place and a place for everything.'

'We can get started.'

MRS CANONICAL
9ᵗʰ November 1888

'Mrs Canonical I presume,' said Shaun, entering the lounge. 'The door was open.'

'I've been expecting you,' said Mrs Canonical. 'You don't mind waiting a few moments do you?'

Adriana blushed red as she exchanged glances with Shaun and then back at the sight of Mrs Canonical reclining in her chair, eyes closed, a small smiled upon her lips, her thighs wide apart, skirts hiked up to her waist, her maid, kneeling between, giving oral pleasure judging by the sounds filling the room.

'I think not,' said Shaun, rolling his shoulders.

Adriana looked sharply at Shaun and then again at Mrs Canonical, as she opened her eyes and looked at them. They were black. Completely black.

'You!' exclaimed Adriana. 'But I banished you.'

The Demon laughed, the harsh guttural laugh startling the maid who looked up in surprised.

'Don't stop!' commanded the Demon. 'You? Banish me? Don't flatter yourself. I chose to leave if you remember.'

'Remove yourself, young woman,' said Shaun.

The maid looked up to her Mistress for instruction.

'You may leave me dear, if you so wish,' said the Demon, in the soft voice of Mrs Canonical.

'Oh no, Mistress, I'll live to obey and worship you.'

'You see my flock loves and worships me.'

Shaun moved into the lounge, pulling the maid, who had returned enthusiastically to her duties, back away from her mistress.

'Leave. Now!'

Adriana reached for her and pulled her gently away.

'Come, it's for the best,' she said.

'Demon! It is time for you to return whence you came,' said Shaun.

Mrs Canonical adjusted her skirts and stood, her actions unhurried, calm, dignified even.

'You and I will face each other soon enough, and then we will see who is the stronger, but that time is not now. For now, I will leave you. This plain is so delightful, so many distractions, so many amusements. I have not had my fill so I will not battle you, you or your little slut.'

Adriana boiled with rage, static crackled all around her, white lightening sparked between her fingertips.

'Oohhhh, I see you are getting stronger, good, this simpering virgin thing you've got going on is tiresome,' said the Demon.

As they watched, black smoke rose, writhing and twisting within its self, from within Mrs Canonical, pooling above her head, as it gained shape and form, two red eyes peering out.

'You will find her none the worse for my passions; I was more along for the ride with this one. Just a little guidance, a little nudge to release her anger was all that was needed.'

Mrs Canonical opened her eyes, which were brown and smiled. She looked up, showing no surprise as the blackness spread its wings, its visage now one of a grotesque caricature of someone once human, once female.

'Begone I say in the name of my Lord, in the Name of my Father, In the Name of my brother, BEGONE.'

Shaun glowed as he stepped forward, his strength in faith, in goodness and peace radiated off him in tangible waves.

Adriana gloried in his presence as tears fell upon her cheeks.

The Demon flinched, and then laughed.

'So strong,' she said. 'I look forward to when we next meet, for should you fall to me, I will have your soul screaming for an eternity.'

Shaun took another step forward, mouth open to renounce the Demon once again when the blackness shrank rapidly, pulling the Demon backwards until it vanished.

Adriana let out a gasp of breath.

'Did you do it? Did you banish it back to hell?'

Shaun shook his head.

'No, like last time, she left of her own accord. We have not seen the last of her.'

Adriana looked at Mrs Canonical.

'Are you ok, Mrs Canonical?'

'Quite fine thank you.'

'Do you know what happened to you?'

Mrs Canonical smiled.

'Oh yes, dear.'

'Would you like to talk about it? Confess? Father Shaun here can take your confession.'

'Confess dear? Sure why not? I killed them. I killed those harlots that stole my husband and son away. I was a little timid at first but Asmodeus showed me the way.'

'Asmodeus!' said Shaun, clearly startled.

'You know of this Demon?' asked Adriana.

Shaun nodded. 'Asmodeus, once an angel, cast out of Heaven by Father.'

Several things clicked into place at once.

'You're an Angel,' said Adriana.

Shaun looked at Adriana, his crooked smile and piercing blue eyes making her heart ache.

'I am.'

Adriana heart sunk. She was in love with an Angel, how could that possibly work.

'Come; let us update Anderson and the rest, so they can send some constables to arrest Mrs Canonical.'

Mrs Canonical seemed untroubled by the prospect and waved them out of the room, a smile upon her lips as she called her maid to her.

'She doesn't look like a woman driven against her will to commit such horrendous acts,' said Adriana, looking over her shoulder as they left.

As Shaun and Adriana crossed the threshold out into the daylight, coldness rippled through them and they found themselves in modern day London.

'Nooooo,' said Adriana in dismay. 'She will get away with it.'

'Come on, let's get back to the office, and check the histories.'

*

'Bother,' said Adriana. 'The Ripper murders are still unsolved.'

Shaun nodded. 'But our theory is further borne out, look.'

Adriana took the sheet of paper.

CASE BOOK: *Jack the Ripper*

'The Pinchin Street Murder,' she read aloud. 'A female torso, covered by an old chemise was discovered under a railway arch in Pinchin Street, missing both legs and the head. So this is similar to the torso found in the basement of the police station a year earlier. This was in September 1889; the first one was October 1888, wasn't it?'

Shaun nodded. 'Keep reading.'

'A man named John Cleary informed the night editor of the New York Herald that there had been a murder in Back Church Lane. Pinchin street runs off of that; and a news vendor claiming to be this John Cleary, said he had been told by a soldier of the murder. John described the man as five foot six, fair complexion, and a moustache, carrying a parcel.'

Adriana looked up at Shaun. 'The small man with the moustache again.'

Shaun nodded.

Adriana read further.

'The abdominal region of the body was heavily mutilated, with the womb missing, reminiscent of the

Ripper. Do you think Mrs Canonical continue killing, even without the influence of the Demon?'

Shaun shook his head. 'No, it says here this body showed no signs of having done manual labour, and despite the papers saying she was a prostitute called Lydia Hart, it was never proven.'

'The date of death is thought to be 8th September 1889, one year after the murder of Annie Chapman.' Adriana read aloud. 'Now, that is interesting, as Annie was the one murder that didn't fit our theory of "Mary."'

Shaun nodded. 'Perhaps the killer we thought responsible for Elisabeth Long, killed Annie Chapman after all.'

'Mrs Canonical, under her demonic influence, copied the Annie Chapman killing? My god, it says here there were other torso killings, one in Rainham in 1887, the Whitechapel torso we are aware of in 1888 and two more in 1889.'

Shaun nodded. 'If our moustache killer is responsible for those *and* Annie Chapman's murder, together with the attack on Ada Wilson, it ties it all up. Also, if this killer is a solider or a sailor it would explain the changes in his complexion, from fair, to dark, or sunburned, as the attack on Ada reported, which always struck me as odd.'

'So the Ripper was in fact two people, working separately but one copying the style of the other to further hide their crimes,' said Adriana. 'One, a woman, killing prostitutes named Mary, seeking Mary Kelly, and another, killing in the most horrendous and grotesque way for reasons we know not what, perhaps just a hatred of women like Aaron Kosminski. Could it be him?'

'Well Assistant Commissioner Anderson and Chief Inspector Swanson certainly thought so,' said Shaun. 'And we know Kosminski was admitted to an Asylum in early 1891 and was transferred to another Asylum in 1894, finally dying in 1919.'

'So the timeline does fit as the murders go as far as 1889 and then stop, he could have done it.'

Shaun nodded. 'Whilst there were a couple of murders that had a tentative Ripperish connection in 1891, after Kosminski was place in an Asylum, the link is tenuous at best.'

'I feel so frustrated,' said Adriana, slamming down the papers onto the desk.

'You sound like Anderson,' said Shaun, with a laugh. 'We released Mrs Canonical from the Demon and her killings certainly seemed to have stopped. The second killer? We know the Demon was moving between the Vicar's maid and Mrs Canonical, perhaps it was also within Kosminski. It would explain his seeming delusions of a higher power talking to him. Perhaps that power was demonic and if he killed Annie Chapman, it would explain the similarities between her murder and the Mary killings.'

Shaun shrugged.

'Even without the demonic influence, the idea of their being two killers, not just one, does have some merit, especially if we take into account the 'Mary' link as a motive. But like so many, it's a theory that I am sure many will enjoy disproving.'

THE END

© 2017 Simon Hartwell

This book is a work of fiction. All characters in the publication are fictitious and any resemblances to real persons, living or dead are purely coincidental.

All rights reserved. This publication (or any part of it) may not be reproduced or transmitted, copied, stored, distributed or otherwise made available by any persons or entity in any form or by any means (photocopying, recording, scanning or otherwise) without prior written permission from Simon Hartwell

Contact

http://simonhartwell.blogspot.co.uk/

simonhartwell@rocketmail.com

Printed in Great Britain
by Amazon